A Gust
of
Wind

LuAnn Henry

ISBN 978-1-64349-398-5 (paperback)
ISBN 978-1-64349-399-2 (digital)

Christian Faith Publishing, Inc.
832 Park Avenue
Meadville, PA 16335
www.christianfaithpublishing.com

Printed in the United States of America

This is a long-time dream that has come to fruition. I am so inspired by many folks, and most of all, I thank my family for their understanding, encouragement, patience, and love.

I have had God in my heart for as long as I can remember. A few years back, I went through a life-changing ordeal. I was on the brink of leaving this world until Jesus spoke to me. I then realized my ordeal led me to an awakening—to a strong, renewed belief in my Lord. I praise the Lord for being there for me then and now.

Family and friends are precious to me and I have now learned that they are dedicated to my love and friendship. My husband, Bob, has always believed in me and has been by my side since we got married in 1975. Thanks to a very dear couple, Craig and Sandi, who encouraged me to follow my dream of writing. Special thanks to my mother who helped me with typing my handwritten manuscript. And I have great appreciation for Samantha, the English teacher who proofed my manuscript and previewed the context of material in my story. She also helped me realize that I truly have a talent to share with those interested in reading.

The story within these pages tells a story of a lady about thirty years of age who is searching for something she is missing in her life. Through the days of finding love, she realizes that she is missing more than a man's love in her life. Her deceased father guides her in the direction to both loves, that of a special man who loves her back and to the love of her Lord in heaven.

I hope and pray that the message in my story helps guide others to the Lord, to know that he can and will help when a person believes in him. I am very blessed and hope all my readers reach the same conclusion in their lives.

Chapter 1

Katrina White couldn't keep her eyes open as the train bounced down the tracks with a rattle and roll in perpetual motion. The hypnotizing motion along with the strange thoughts provoking her mind gave a gentle lull as her head started to drop to her shoulder and her hands in her lap became limber and shook with the motion of the train. As she drifted off to a light sleep, she started to dream of a handsome man standing next to a beautiful Appaloosa horse. She didn't recognize the dark-toned face with brown eyes, the long shoulder-length dark brown hair with golden streaks pulled back, or the slender, well-toned body. When the horse started to move, Katrina was jarred awake. She looked around to see what was going on, her eyes stopped and gazed at the back of the train car. There sitting in the last seat was a man who resembled the man in her dream. She rubbed her eyes in disbelief. She figured she must have seen him on the train before she dreamt about him. How else could she have had the same man in her dream? This really puzzled her.

She turned back toward the window and looked out at the green field with tiny, white flowers splattered throughout. What a beautiful sight! In the background were a few rolling hills with a backdrop of blue sky holding white billowing puffs of clouds. Once again, she closed her eyes and started to drift off to sleep.

The whistle was blowing long with a sharp piercing tone; she was jolted awake. This time she realized that the train had stopped and that people were getting off. The conductor was coming through the back door when she heard him say, "Last stop before we get to Widow's Peak. There are no facilities for food or lodging, but there is a place to freshen up. We leave in fifteen minutes."

Katrina hadn't thought about food or drink for quite a while. She did know that she needed to step out for a minute. As she stood, she turned around and noticed the man in the last seat was gone. She made her way to the front of the car and out the door. Just as she was stepping down from the train car, a hand reached out to her. She looked up and there was the same man whom she noticed before. She reached her hand out and said, "Thank you. This step is rather high." As her hand touched his, she felt the roughness of his fingers with a firm grip wrapping around her palm. She didn't dare look up for fear of swooning since he was a very attractive man. Once she was firmly on the platform, she quickly glanced up at him with a brief smile and turned away as she pulled her hand from his.

"You are very welcome, ma'am," were the words that came from his lips with a very soft yet raspy voice. She didn't dare turn to look at him again. There was something about him. She couldn't pinpoint it, but he made her feel strange.

She wondered if he was watching her as she walked away. "Don't be silly," she muttered under her breath. "What has come over you?"

The outhouse had a line waiting. Katrina figured this would be a good time to stretch her legs. She saw a fence just past a barn not far from the outhouse. She thought, *I wonder if there are any horses and cows behind the barn?* She strolled over to the fence and peered around the barn. No animals in sight. That seemed strange. She wondered where they were. Just then a tiny kitten darted toward her and ran up to her, rubbing up against her leg and foot. *What a cute kitten*, thought Katrina. She bent down to pet the yellow tiger-looking kitten. The kitten purred very loud and continued to go back and forth against Katrina's leg and foot.

A voice from behind her startled her. "I think the kitten likes you." It was that voice again. Without turning around, she remarked, "I believe so." Katrina stood up and looked back. There he was standing and watching her. She quickly glanced around him and noticed that the line had only a couple of folks standing in front of the outhouse.

"Excuse me," said Katrina as she attempted to quickly skirt around him and head to the outhouse to get in the shortened line.

She didn't dare turn around. There was a petite girl in a blue dress with a matching bonnet in front of her. The child looked around and then looked up at Katrina. Katrina smiled when she noticed the little face with freckles and blue eyes. The girl's red ringlets were pushing out of her bonnet and springing every which way around the peach-colored face. *What a sweet little girl*, thought Katrina. Just then an aged man stepped out of the outbuilding and was wiping his nose with a hankie. The little girl stepped into the building and closed the door. It seemed like eternity. The train whistle started to blow. Just then the door opened, and the freckled face was crying.

"What is the matter, little one?" inquired Katrina.

The girl looked up and sobbed the words, "I can't pull my dress down all the way."

"Here, let me help you," offered Katrina. The little one turned sideways as Katrina realized her petticoat was tucked up in her pantaloons. Katrina squatted down and pulled the petticoat out and smoothed it down as she said, "There, you are all set. Now you don't have to cry."

"Thank you, miss," responded the girl as she started to run toward the train.

Katrina quickly went into the outbuilding with no time to waste and was back on the train just as the whistle started to blow again. Once back in the car, she looked around for a place to sit. Most people were in the same seats they were in before the train stopped. As she counted seats to find the one she was in, she realized that there was someone different sitting behind her. It was him. She wondered if she should find another seat. Then she thought, *What am I doing? I don't know him, and he means nothing to me*. Katrina sat in the exact same seat she was in before. As she was getting settled, she began to panic. *Was this guy stalking me?* she said in her head. Then she could feel her cheeks grow warm. *This is not the time to blush*, she thought. *What is going through my head? Stop it!* she screamed to herself. *Just close your eyes and go back to sleep. It's a long ride ahead*. Slowly she drifted off to sleep again.

Chapter 2

Once again Katrina awakened to the train whistle. She couldn't believe she had slept the rest of the journey. The train was pulling into Widow's Peak station. As the train went slowly past the first street, Katrina noticed several buildings on both sides of the street. There was a one-story building with a sign in front that said "Wally's General Store." Another building had a sign shaped like a tooth, and next to that one was a two-story building that had a large front entrance and a white railing porch on the first and second floor of the front of the green-painted building. There was no sign to tell what the proprietary type was. Across the street, she noticed a large building that appeared to be the town saloon. The next street came into view before she could see any more of the first street. The second street was where the train came to a stop, and the train station was on the far side. Katrina noticed the sheriff's office and another small building that had a sign for a doctor. Just past that was a dress shop, and at the end of the street was a white building with a steeple that she believed was the church.

The conductor announced, "Last stop. Widow's Peak. All to depart, as the train is shutting down for the night."

Katrina thought that was strange for the train to not go on. She did see the water tower and thought maybe they had to wait to take on water or get wood.

As Katrina stepped down from the train, she noticed the little girl with the blue bonnet run into the arms of an older woman with a beautiful baby blue day dress and blue bonnet. The woman had curly hair just like the girl. *Maybe it is her mother*, thought Katrina. Then she noticed the handsome man from the train approach the woman, and the two embraced. She saw the woman smile at the man then turn to hug the girl. The man then gave the little girl a hug and walked away, leaving the two standing there and watching him leave. When the lady turned around, she noticed Katrina watching them. She started to approach Katrina. Katrina felt awkward and turned to enter the train station.

Upon entering the first room in the station, Katrina noticed the room was small but held a couple of chairs and a small table against one wall, and the opposite wall had a clock and a large blackboard with several names of destinations and times. The wall across from the door where she stood held a barred window showing another room in the back and an old man with whiskers standing behind it. The sign above read "Station Manager." He was stamping papers for a gray-haired lady in a green travel coat who had just departed from the train. While Katrina was glancing around noticing the room, the lady with the sweet little girl entered and walked up to the window.

Katrina heard the older lady say that she wanted to hire a driver to take her to the Whitaker Ranch. The station manager pointed to a man entering the building. It was him again. Katrina started to feel flushed in the face again and tingly in her legs. *Stop it,* Katrina said to herself mentally.

The gray-haired lady approached the man as he ambled in. "I understand you can drive me to the Whitaker Ranch?" It was half a statement and half a question from the woman to her mystery man.

"Yes, I can." As he responded, he looked at Katrina. "Is there anyone else who needs a ride that way?" He then looked around the room. There was a chubby middle-aged man standing by the message board carrying a black bag and wearing a plaid overcoat.

"I certainly can use a ride. Are you by chance going past the Martin place?" asked the business-looking man.

Katrina looked startled. She repeated in her head, *The Martin homestead?* That's where she was headed. She wondered what he wanted there. She hesitated to say anything, and just then her mystery man responded, "Yes, I am driving close by there and can detour the extra five miles. It's really not out of the way."

She didn't want to say anything. She wasn't sure she wanted to ride with him. Then she wondered how far it was and thought he might be the only way out to the homestead. So, she mustered her courage and said, "I am also going to the Martin homestead."

The businessman looked at her and asked, "Are you family to the Martin's?"

Katrina wasn't sure if she should tell him or not. She hesitated for a few seconds then responded in a hushed tone, "Maybe. Maybe not." She turned to her mystery man and asked when he was planning to head out.

He responded, "As soon as everyone is ready. My wagon will be waiting just out this door." He pointed to a door next to the station manager's window. At that time, he walked across the room and left through that same door.

Just then a young boy about sixteen years of age entered by the front door and said the luggage was sitting on the front porch. "Please pick up yar baggage quickly as I don't hold to bein' responsibly for yar stuff."

The businessman quickly shuffled his way out the door, and the older woman followed suit. Katrina waited for them to go through the doorway then she exited the building. She looked for her bags and couldn't find them. She panicked. *Where did they go?* she wondered. Just then she saw the handsome mystery man come around the building and step onto the porch and pick up three bags. The older woman said, "Oh, thank you for getting my bags. I appreciate such a kind young man helping." She followed him to the side of the building. The businessman picked up his one bag and followed also. Katrina stood there confused and looked under the bench then along the wall just as her mystery man came back around the train station.

"I have your bags already loaded in the wagon, miss." He reached out to her as if he was going to take her hand. Once again Katrina could feel her face turn warm. She knew her cheeks were becoming a soft pink color. She decided to not take his hand. She knew she would just melt if she did. She hiked up her skirt just enough so she wouldn't trip and quickly stepped past him and around the corner. There was the wagon with the other two folks sitting in the second seat. Katrina noticed the little girl from the train sitting in between them. She wondered if the older lady was the grandmother to the girl.

Then it dawned on Katrina. Where will she be sitting? Her thought went to *No, not in the first seat with the driver, with the man that made her quiver in her shoes.* She realized she didn't have a choice, and she didn't want to make a fuss. As she approached the wagon, she felt his presence behind her.

"Here, let me help you up," he stated as she could almost feel his breath on her neck. She hesitated then decided she didn't want to make a scene. She lifted her right foot up onto the wheel hub just as he put his arm around her waist. She felt as light as a feather as he hoisted her up and gently placed her on the seat. Then he climbed up next to her as she slid over to make room for him and to sit as close to the other side of the seat as she could get. She scooped her skirting and tucked it under her legs as she whispered, "Thank you."

Katrina kept her eyes straight ahead as the wagon started to roll forward. She hoped that he didn't make chitchat during the ride.

"How far is the Whitaker Ranch, sir?" asked the little girl.

"It's about ten miles. And please call me Jack." He turned to look at her and winked and gave her a big smile. He added, "We will have to get going as we will have to go around Widow's Peak to get there so it will take longer."

The businessman responded, "I thought that was the town's name. And by the way, I'm Raymond."

Jack replied, "It is. It's named for the peak that we will go around. Nice to meet you, Raymond." Jack turned his head and tipped his hat toward Raymond.

The older lady then stated, "I'm Mrs. Beechwood. I have been entrusted to bring this young lady, Elizabeth, home. She is the daughter to Mr. Whitaker. She has been away to school, and her father wanted her to come home and continue her studies there."

Jack turned and removed his hat. "It's a pleasure to see you, Lizzy." He winked his right eye as he looked at her. Then he turned his head slightly. "And you as well, Mrs. Beechwood. I am sure Mr. Whitaker is anxiously awaiting your arrival."

"Yes, he is," remarked Mrs. Beechwood. "I hate to ask this, but is it possible that you can take us there first?" She nodded her head toward Katrina and Raymond as she continued to say, "I wouldn't want Mr. Whitaker worrying about when we will be arriving."

"I could, as long as Raymond and . . . I don't believe we have heard your name." He looked at Katrina and waited for an answer.

Hesitantly, she responded, "Katrina Martin."

Raymond spoke up after hearing her name. "I don't mind the wait, as long as Miss Martin doesn't mind."

Katrina wondered why he didn't question her more about being family from the Martin homestead. Why was he going there? It didn't cross her mind until now to even question it when he stated his destination. This left her puzzled and thinking until she heard, "Miss Martin, do you hear me?" inquired Jack.

Katrina then realized that she was being spoken to and turned toward Jack. "I'm sorry. I was thinking."

"I wanted to know what you want to do, Miss Martin. Okay to take the little one home first?" Jack said in a sincere and caring voice.

Katrina thought quickly, *Do I want to take the whole ride with him? But then that's not fair to the little girl who is surely anxiously waiting to see her family.* "That will be fine." Katrina was surprised to hear that come from her so quickly and agreeably.

"Then that's what we shall do," replied Jack as he cracked the reins for the horses to gallop quickly. Katrina held on to the seat as best as she could so as not to bounce around too much. She wondered why he was in such a hurry.

Then Mrs. Beechwood remarked, "Slow down some please. You are throwing us around like bouncing balls." Elizabeth giggled as she was holding on to Mrs. Beechwood and Raymond.

"This is fun," stated Elizabeth as she continued to giggle.

Mrs. Beechwood replied, "Only if you aren't a mess when your father sees you." She was hanging on to the edge of her seat with one hand and holding on to Elizabeth with the other hand.

Jack then responded, "I'm truly sorry but it will soon be night and we need to get to our destination before nightfall."

Raymond then asked, "What's the concern?"

Jack replied as he continued to hurry the horses, "There are wolves and bears that come out at night, and it gets rather cool. It will certainly not be the proper place for womenfolk."

Lizzy leaned toward Mrs. Beechwood and clasped her coat with fear in her eyes.

"Now see what you have done, Jack. You have put fear into this child!" exclaimed Mrs. Beechwood. Turning toward Lizzy, she cupped her face with one hand while still hanging on to the seat with the other. "Do not fear, my little one. Jack will not let anything get to us."

Raymond then asked, "Will we continue our journey tonight after reaching the Whitaker Ranch?"

"No, we will have to spend the night then leave after breakfast. Mr. Whitaker is a gracious host and won't mind, especially if we get his little girl to him tonight." Jack looked straight over the horses, concentrating on the road.

Katrina was somewhat glad that Jack had to concentrate to make the arrival safe and sound tonight. She hoped that the conversations would now stop going back and forth. She wasn't used to so much talking. Maybe now she could think back to why Raymond was heading to the Martin farm. She thought about her past correspondence with her uncle. He didn't say anything about a businessman coming to the farm or about the farm being in any trouble.

Is that what it could be? Was the farm in trouble? Was it financial trouble? Was Uncle Tom going to sell the farm? Oh no! She hoped that wasn't the case. She had come so far to be at the farm. She was so hoping that this change in location could help her move on in her life. What was she up against? Did she think this trip through well enough? Maybe she should have wired Uncle Tom about her arrival. She was sure he wouldn't mind her being there. Was she too presumptuous?

Katrina felt a hand grasp her arm. It jolted her from her thoughts. She realized that they had turned a sharp corner and she was leaning partway out of the wagon.

"Whoa, there. Hang on, Miss Martin. We would hate to dump you here in the middle of nowhere," remarked Jack. It was Jack's hand on her arm. She began to feel the warmth in her face. She reprimanded herself in her mind. *Silly girl. Pay attention.*

"I'm okay," stated Katrina as she pulled herself back in position and moved her arm from this man next to her, hoping he would let go of her arm.

"We don't want to lose you." Lizzy snickered, who thought the whole ride was an extraordinary experience. "I like fast rides."

At this point, Katrina thought it best to pay attention to the road and the drive so she wasn't caught off guard again.

The air started to turn to a brisk coolness. Katrina realized this and wished she had put her shawl on. Without realizing it, she clutched her arms and started to rub her shoulders for warmth. Jack noticed this as he glanced toward her and wondered if he should stop so she could get something out of her bag for warmth. Then he thought it would only be another hour and then they would reach the ranch. He looked back at the others, and they were wearing coats and appeared comfortable. Jack decided to continue riding on.

Katrina wondered if Jack was cold. She saw that he didn't have a coat and the shirt he was wearing was not very thick. She thought, *Does he own a coat? Does he travel all the time?* She wondered if he had any family and if he had a sweetheart. Here she goes again. Not paying attention to the road. But those thoughts did warm her up some as she wasn't thinking about the cold.

As they rode up to a pathway with small dangling willow trees on each side of it, Katrina noticed a big white, two-story house with a large veranda on the side and an ivy-drenched coating and a pillared porch in the front. She thought the house to be out of place. She had heard of such places in the south but didn't know they existed in the west. To the right of the veranda, she saw a white picket fence with colors of the rainbow on the other side. It must be their flower yard. At least that's what she called the gardens back home. She could see there were archways throughout the garden with all kinds of flowers climbing on them—beautiful red and yellow roses, purple wisteria, and orange trumpet flowers.

The front double doors of the house opened as a tall man and a boy who appeared to be about twelve stepped out and marched down the steps. Jack brought the wagon around to the hitching post in front of the steps and came to a stop. He jumped off the wagon while still holding the reins and walked around the horses. He tied the reins to the hitching post and walked around to the other side of the wagon to greet the man and boy by shaking their hands. There appeared to be quiet conversation between them, and then the man of the house stepped towards the wagon and assisted Mrs. Beechwood down. Once she was firmly planted on the ground, Mr. Whitaker turned to help Lizzy down. She jumped into his arms and hugged him tightly around the neck.

"Oh, Poppa, it is so good to see you. If you only knew how much I have missed you. I am so glad to be home," the excited little girl stated as she continued to have a firm, grasping hug with this man she called Poppa.

"Now, Lizzy, you still talk too much," Poppa responded with a puckering kiss on her cheek. "And I have missed you so much, my little princess."

The boy came forward and grabbed Lizzy by the shoulders and leaned her toward him. "Did you miss me too, little sister?"

"Oh no, Johnny, 'cause I know you didn't miss me," responded Lizzy with a giggle and her hand covering her mouth.

"Yes, I missed picking on you, you little munchkin." Johnny pulled a ringlet then turned to run away.

At that time, Mr. Whitaker let Lizzy down, and she chased Johnny into the house. Mrs. Beechwood followed as she called out to Lizzy, "Little girls don't run, Elizabeth."

Mr. Whitaker then turned to Jack. "You might as well stay the night than to travel on and take a chill." At the same time, Mr. Whitaker went over to reach up to Katrina. "May I help you down, ma'am? You'll spend the night, and Jack will take you in the morning to the Martin farm."

Katrina reached out to accept his hand and sprang down from the wagon as graciously as she could. At the same time, Raymond climbed down the wagon from the other side. Raymond and Jack grabbed the baggage to take into the house. Another man came from the stables down the pathway from the house. This man unhitched the horses to take them to the stables for the night. Katrina attempted to grab one of her bags when Jack responded that he had them and would take them inside.

Mr. Whitaker took Katrina's arm and remarked, "This way my dear. I am so very glad to have company, especially one so pretty." His smile was genuine, and he seemed such a gentleman to Katrina so she allowed him to escort her inside.

Upon entering the main room, Katrina knew her mouth was open, and just as quickly as she realized it, she closed it. The room was white and spacious with a spiral staircase to the right of the room. The staircase went up to an open balcony that spanned the entire opposite side of the staircase. A huge chandelier hung in the center of the domed ceiling. There were murals on the wall to the other side of the staircase. Several doors led to other rooms off this main room, and a hallway went straight to the back of the house, with several doors exiting from the hall.

A young girl in a plain black dress with a white apron came to take the coats. She went into a room off the hallway and quickly returned. The whole time she didn't say a word. Just then Katrina heard footsteps on the balcony and saw Lizzy peering over the railing.

"Poppa, I forgot how beautiful everything is here. I am so glad to be home!" exclaimed Lizzy as she disappeared from the railing.

Mr. Whitaker looked at Katrina and said, "You must be exhausted after your trip. Amelia will show you to your room. Are you a relative to Tom Martin?"

Amelia was the young girl with the apron. She looked at Jack, and he pointed to Katrina's baggage. Amelia grabbed a bag, and Jack grabbed the other two.

"Why do you ask that?" asked Katrina as she stepped back.

And just then Jack said, "This way to your room."

Katrina was relieved as she didn't want to get into a conversation about herself. She followed Jack up the stairs. Jack seemed to know where he was going, which Katrina suddenly realized as he entered the second door at the top of the stairs. Jack set the bags down and took the one from Amelia and sat that one next to the others. He then went further into the room and found a lamp, lit it, and replaced the glass as he turned and looked at her.

Once again, Katrina felt flushed as she stood just inside the doorway. She wished the windows were open so she could feel a breeze to cool her face. Katrina walked into the room and stated, "Thank you for your assistance."

Jack knew she must be tired, and he replied, "You're welcome," as he exited the room and closed the door.

The next morning, Katrina awoke to the sun shining in the windows. She panicked to the thought of the time and wondered if she had overslept. She admitted to herself that she did have a good night's sleep in the comfort of the downy bed and the soft, warm quilt on top of her. She crawled out of bed and found a washbowl filled with water and fluffy towels next to it. As she touched the water, she noticed that it was still warm. It couldn't have been brought in that long ago. She thought, *Must be Amelia brought it in.* She quickly washed up and got dressed then went to the bed to pull the quilt up and smooth out the bed to look as nice as it did before she slept in it.

There was a knock at the door. Mrs. Beechwood asked her if she was ready for breakfast right after knocking. Katrina responded with a yes as her stomach growled. She suddenly realized she hadn't eaten since yesterday morning. Katrina stepped out onto the stairway balcony and then remembered the beautiful area downstairs that she saw last night. She slowly walked down the staircase as she was thinking about how lovely it would be to get married in a place like this. She thought it would be like living in a palace like she read about in books. As Katrina reached the bottom step, Lizzy came bounding down the stairs and flew past Katrina.

Lizzy called back, "Last one to the table has to clean up!"

Johnny walked in from the front door at the same time, saw Lizzy, and heard her, then he took off toward the hallway, stating, "That will be you, not me," as he looked at Katrina with a smile.

Katrina followed Johnny into the dining room. Once again, her mouth felt like it hit the floor, and she closed it quickly. As she looked around, she thought this room to be very exquisite. Just then

Johnny said, "We don't always eat in here unless we have guests. This is a privilege."

Johnny sat down near the head of the table next to Mr. Whitaker. Katrina then wondered if Johnny was Mr. Whitaker's son. She assumed so based on how Johnny and Lizzy reacted to each other. Mrs. Beechwood was sitting next to Lizzy on the other side of the table. Raymond hadn't come down yet apparently and Jack was sitting at the other end of the table.

Mrs. Beechwood pulled the chair out next to her and said, "Sit here, dearie." Katrina hesitated. Sitting near Mrs. Beechwood would mean that she would be sitting next to Jack. She would much rather sit on the other side where there was more room. But then she thought against it as she figured there was a reason for her to sit on the side with the women. She didn't want to offend anyone. Katrina sat down just as Raymond came into the room and took the seat next to Johnny. Amelia walked in with a couple of trays full of breakfast foods that smelled wonderful. With a tray in each hand, Amelia gracefully set them on the buffet. Again, Katrina's stomach gurgled, and she so hoped that no one heard.

As everyone finished breakfast and started to get up, Jack said to Mr. Whitaker, "Thank you for breakfast. I must get Miss Martin and Raymond out to the Martin farm."

Raymond responded, "Yes, thank you for your wonderful hospitality. I certainly had a great night's sleep, and this meal was superb." He stood up and bowed to the ladies then turned to leave the room.

Mr. Whitaker looked at Katrina as she stood up. "Miss Martin, are you related to Tom Martin over the hill?"

Katrina knew she had to answer, but she didn't want these folks to know much about her. Why did she want to keep quiet about herself? She couldn't figure out what she was up to and knew she had to think this through on the way to the farm.

"I am." Is that all she was going to say? Mr. Whitaker deserved to know a little bit more about her. It sounded like he knew her uncle. "He's my uncle." There, that was enough to be told, and she wasn't being ignorant toward him. She started to walk out of the room as Mr. Whitaker replied, "Please be sure to tell your uncle I send my best and that I hope to get out there to see him soon."

Katrina turned briefly and nodded her head, and then she left the room. As she approached the main room, she noticed her bags were already brought down. Just then, Johnny picked them up and carried them out the door. Lizzy came from another door next to the staircase and stopped in front of Katrina.

"Miss Martin, will I see you again?" asked Lizzy.

Jack came from the hallway. He walked over to Lizzy, and as he tugged on one of her ringlets, he answered, "We hope so, Lizzy. She will be just over the hill from us." He turned to Katrina and said, "It's time to go." Jack then walked out the front door. Katrina wondered why he didn't offer to assist her like a gentleman would. Then she thought, *why would she expect him to do that?* She noticed that Lizzy had already left the room, and Katrina walked out the door to the wagon.

Raymond was already in the front seat. Katrina felt relieved that she wouldn't have to ride in the front with Jack. Jack assisted her into the second seat then climbed into the driver's seat, and off they went. It seemed like hours that they were riding around the hill when they came upon a farm house with two big barns and pastures that seemed to go way behind the barns, and there were trees throughout the pasture and a small set of woods to the left of the farmhouse. The farmhouse was a simple one-story structure with a full front porch that held tree-cut railings that were entwined with brambles. Smoke was billowing out of the chimney that reached above the roof and silhouetted an oak tree standing nearby the house.

As they approached the farm, Katrina was also noticing that the barn roof had recently been repaired with fresh cut lumber, and there was a new double door on the side that was an entrance to a split-rail, fenced-in corral. Beyond the corral was another wooden fence that ran directly back to the edge of a set of woods and continued alongside the woods until it disappeared behind the barn.

The wagon came to a stop in front of the house.

Chapter 3

As Katrina walked toward the front door, she felt a soft breeze and noticed a cardinal in the tall pine tree near the house. The front door opened, and out walked a man in his fifties with graying hair that was receding and eyes that were a bright blue.

"Hi, folks, glad to see you. I'm Tom Martin," said the man who walked out the door at the same time the cardinal flew away. Tom stepped down from the porch and walked up to Katrina and held out his hand. "Katrina, I didn't know you were coming now. I am so glad to see you."

Katrina smiled and extended her hand to him then went into a full hug with Tom. "Uncle Tom, it is good to see you."

At that point, Uncle Tom looked over at Raymond. "Are you here about the land, sir?" asked Uncle Tom.

Raymond walked over to Tom and extended his hand, "I'm Raymond Coats. I am here to find out about the land and what we can do to help." Raymond then put his other hand on top of Tom Martin's hand that he was shaking. Tom let go and dropped his arms to his side. "Mr. Coats, I am afraid there has been a miscommunication. My land is fine, and I don't need your help."

Katrina wondered what they were talking about. What was Mr. Coats doing here? What did Uncle Tom do or didn't do about the land? Was it too late for her to be here? She couldn't think that. This was her world now, and she needed this world. She couldn't lose it now that she was here. She felt a wave of panic flow over her, and just then she felt a gust of wind. There was a warming flow of air that waved past her and then was gone. Then she felt weak in the knees.

Suddenly she was lying on a bed. The room was small and had one tall chest of drawers, a nightstand with a kerosene lamp, and the large bed she was on. Behind the door was a series of hooks with nothing hanging on them. The chest of drawers was barren on top. There was one picture on the wall, and that was a picture of Jesus. With the sun shining in the window, she felt the room was cheery on its own despite the emptiness of the room. She noticed the wallpaper was of pink roses and green leaves that held a uniform pattern all over the walls. No one was in the room. She heard voices in another room. She managed to get out of the bed and walked to the doorway.

Tom Martin was pouring coffee into several cups when he noticed Katrina in the doorway. "Come in, honey. I hope you are all right. The trip must have been too much for you."

Jack pulled out the chair closest to where Katrina stood. "Here, have a seat." Katrina went to the chair and sat. Jack pushed her in toward the table then proceeded to sit next to her. "Are you okay? You gave us a quite a scare."

Katrina smiled and, looking at her uncle, said, "I'm fine, thank you." She reached for an empty cup. Tom saw this and leaned over to pour coffee into the cup just as Katrina put her hand over the top of the cup. "I would prefer some tea, if you have it, Uncle Tom." Tom looked up from his task and looked toward the wall cupboard. "I don't believe I do, honey. But I will pick some up the next time I'm in town. Okay?" Katrina nodded and turned the cup over on the table. Uncle Tom picked the cup up and went to the hand pump on the cabinet and filled the cup with water. He then returned to the table and placed the cup in front of Katrina. "Here's some nice cold water for now." Katrina took the cup and sipped some water then placed the cup back on the table. "Thank you, Uncle Tom."

Katrina wondered what was talked about when she fainted. Did the men talk business? Why was Jack still here? He never mentioned knowing her uncle during the trip from the train. Katrina was puzzled, and it showed on her face.

"Is everything okay?" asked Uncle Tom. "I know this place isn't what you were expecting, but it's all your dad and I have left."

That was the first time in a long time that anyone mentioned her father. She wondered what he was really like. Was he like Uncle Tom? Did he really grow up in this house with parents and a brother and sister? She had so many questions to ask but didn't dare while the other two men were present. It would have to wait until it was just her and her uncle. That way they could talk without interruptions and without others knowing their family business. She wished she knew more about the Martin family and the farm. She wondered how Uncle Tom ran the place by himself. Maybe it wasn't a working farm anymore. Maybe that is why Raymond was here. Katrina thought, *Enough second guessing.* Right now, she wanted so much to wander around and see things.

Raymond was sitting at the table working on papers, and Uncle Tom went over to the fireplace to build up the fire. Jack was still sitting next to her but was looking at the papers Raymond was working on. This made it even more puzzling. Why was Jack looking at the papers? Who were they for? Jack turned and looked at Katrina. He saw that she was puzzled about something and noticed that she was looking at the papers.

"We're working on a contract," stated Jack as if to answer her unspoken question.

Katrina stood up and took her cup to the sink. Then she proceeded to walk over to her uncle. "Uncle Tom, what is going on?" She placed both her hands on the spindle-pointed top of Uncle Tom's chair. She decided she might need the support.

Uncle Tom looked at her with sad eyes, a frown, and a wrinkled brow and took her hands in his. "Dear, Katrina, you came so far. I didn't believe you would ever come here. I had to take action or lose the farm completely."

Katrina dropped her hands and with a surprised look questioned her uncle, "What are you talking about . . . losing the farm? What has happened?" She turned to look at Jack and Raymond. "Just what is going on?" she questioned in a stern tone and with glaring eyes. She did all she could to hold back the tears.

Jack stood up and started to walk toward her. "Katrina, your uncle doesn't have any money to keep the farm going. The farm isn't making any money, and the bank has threatened to take the land."

Uncle Tom interrupted, "Jack, it's for me to tell her." Uncle Tom took a hold of Katrina's arm and turned her toward him. "My dear, I am selling the land to Jack. He will own the farm." Katrina looked at her uncle then at Jack.

"No," cried Katrina. She didn't know what to say or do at this point. What was going on? She had come so far, and now what she thought was going to be her life was being pulled out from under her. She felt weak in the knees. She didn't want to faint, not again. She turned and ran out the door as fast as she could. She ran to the barn, and then she went past the barn and noticed a set of woods to the left of the pasture and kept running. When she came to the edge of the trees, she noticed that there were beautiful yellow and brown flowers spread throughout the edging of the woods. *Brown-eyed Susan's*, she thought. They are so bright with color. They were like a ray of sunshine. She smiled. It would have been nice to pick some and put them in a vase on the table. No need to give that another thought since the table wasn't hers, the flowers weren't hers, neither was the farm. She slowed down and walked the tree line. She noticed a lovely small pond just a short distance to her left. *This is a beautiful farm,* she thought. *I want this farm.* Katrina realized that she had to take quick action and figure out how she could help her uncle keep the farm. She then decided she needed to go into town. Strolling back to the house, she tried to sort things out in her head, but she was still very confused.

As Katrina entered the house, everyone in the room looked at her. She looked at Jack and asked him, "Will you take me in to town?"

Jack looked at her uncle then back at her, "Sure, when do you want to go?"

"As soon as I can," remarked Katrina as she cocked her head to one side and looked at her uncle. "Uncle Tom, I need to check on some things."

"I . . . I don't know what to say or do, Katrina. What can I do?" asked Uncle Tom with a sullen face. His hands were resting on the table in prayer formation.

"Give me some time, please," stated Katrina as she picked up her handbag and headed to the door. She turned to look at her uncle. "Can you please give me some time before signing any papers?"

"I will give you time, Katrina. Do you think you can do anything? What do you have in mind?" questioned Uncle Tom.

Katrina looked at Uncle Tom and said, "I will let you know as soon as I know." Katrina turned and walked out the door toward the wagon. She was hoping that Jack was following her as she wanted to leave right away. She climbed into the second seat of the wagon and situated herself before she looked up to see that Jack was getting in the front seat.

It was a very quiet ride as they drove out of sight of the house. Jack wasn't sure whether to talk or not. He wondered what this young woman had on her mind. Was she able to do something about her uncle's land? His thoughts trailed off as they rounded the bend of Widow's Peak.

Katrina felt it was wise to not say anything. She was afraid she would say too much to this man who was willing to take her uncle's land away. She knew she had to get to the telegraph office and send a message to Jeremy Post. He would be able to tell her what she needs to do.

As they approached town, Jack looked back at Katrina. "Where do you need to go?" he asked her.

"The telegraph office, please," said Katrina.

Jack pulled up to the train station and stopped the wagon. "The station manager will be able to help you. He is our telegrapher. I will wait for you."

"Thank you," replied Katrina and she started to get out of the wagon. Jack jumped down from the wagon and jogged around to her side and extended his hand to her to assist her in getting out. Katrina took his hand as she knew that he was offering a gentleman's gesture. Katrina entered the building and walked over to the barred window that she saw when she got off the train.

The station manager was sorting papers on a table and looked up as she came near the window. "How may I help you, ma'am?"

"I would like to send a telegram. May I have a piece of paper?" stated Katrina.

Jack walked into the building at that time. "Miss Katrina, I will be back in a few minutes. When you are done, you can wait by the wagon."

"Thank you," replied Katrina as she turned briefly to acknowledge Jack, and then she turned back around as the manager handed her paper and pencil. She replied to the manager, "Thank you."

Katrina took the paper and pencil and started writing as Jack closed the door behind him as he left the building.

Katrina was starting to pay the station manager for the telegraph when Jack walked into the train station. Katrina reached into her purse and handed the manager some coins. "Is there a way I can get my answer delivered to the Martin farm when it is returned? I would like a confidential reply."

The station manager looked at Jack then back at Katrina. "Yes, I have a young boy who delivers for me. I will have him ride out with your message as soon as I get it." The manager placed the coins in a drawer and walked over to the telegraph machine and started punching the machine with long and short spurts. Katrina then wondered if Jack knew Morse code. She was done anyway and decided not to linger any longer. She turned and walked past Jack and out the door. Jack started to walk toward the manager. Katrina noticed this and decided to attempt to distract him. "Jack, where is the bank?"

Jack was startled to hear her ask him a question. He was more startled when she asked about the bank. He wondered what she was up to. "Follow me and I will show you where the bank is," replied a puzzled Jack. He walked toward her and opened the door and stepped aside so she could go through as he held the door open. Katrina made her way past Jack and waited for him to tell her which way to go to get to the bank. As Jack went through the door and closed it, he placed his hand in the center of Katrina's back to guide her. This startled her, and she tried to pull away. Jack took his hand away as Katrina started walking in front of him. As he pulled his hand away, he raised his other hand and pointed to the bank. Jack wasn't sure if he should escort her to the bank or stand by the wagon. Jack decided to stand by the wagon and wait as he was learning that she was a very independent lady.

When Katrina entered the bank, she turned and noticed that Jack stayed by the wagon. *Good,* she thought. She would be able to take care of business without him looking over her shoulder. She quickly completed her transaction.

As Katrina walked back to the wagon where Jack was waiting, she noticed he was leaning against the wagon wheel with his silver-decorated hat pulled down over part of his face. She wondered what Jack really was doing and who he was. He seemed to be such a puzzle to her.

As she approached the wagon, he sensed her being near and raised his hat and head to see her coming. He reached out his hand to help her climb onto the wagon. She automatically grabbed his arm and hoisted herself up into the seat. As she sat down, she realized she was in the front seat and Jack had climbed up and was sitting next to her. She hoped that he wasn't going to ask questions. She didn't want to tell him anything of her thoughts and plans.

As they rode back to the farm, there was complete silence except for the clippety-clop sound coming from the hooves of the horses. Partway back, Katrina realized that the deafening sound of nothing was making her irritated. She wished that she didn't feel so strange when she was near this man. She thought that there was something special about him. But she couldn't quite put her fingers on it. She knew he was very handsome, he was a gentleman, and he wanted her uncle's ranch. Wait, he was after her ranch! She felt like the wind was just taken from her chest. She started gasping and coughing.

Jack heard Katrina cough. He looked directly at her as he asked, "Are you okay?"

Katrina drew in a deep breath then she replied, "I'm fine," as she worked on gaining her composure. She covered her mouth as she drew in a deep breath.

The horses came to an abrupt halt from Jack yanking back on the reins. He turned toward Katrina. "Are you sure you're okay?"

With another deep breath, Katrina nodded her head up and down. She placed her hand over her throat. "I'm fine. Just took in too much air, I guess." She knew that wasn't what it was, but she also knew she couldn't tell him what was on her mind. There was too much to learn first, and she didn't know where things were going. She decided a white lie was safe. Suddenly she looked up in the sky and said a silent prayer of forgiveness to the Lord. Just then there was a soft gentle breeze that made her feel comfortable.

Chapter 4

Back at the farm, Uncle Tom came out of the barn just as Jack and Katrina pulled up in the wagon. He closed the doors to the barn and turned to see Jack helping Katrina from the wagon. He smiled slightly and thought that it would be nice if there was a relationship with the two of them. He said a simple prayer: "Lord, please help them to find each other."

Katrina walked over to her uncle and put her arm around him. "Uncle Tom, you work too hard. Let me help you. Please?" She wove her arm around his waist and walked with him back to the house. Inside, Katrina took the kettle and filled it with water. As she walked over to the stove, Jack entered the room.

"Tom, I have to go home. I will be back in the morning to help with the fence mending." Jack looked at Katrina, and there was a flash in his mind wondering if this would be what it was like if she stays. Jack went to walk out the door when Tom said, "Jack, I will definitely need your help tomorrow. See ya in the morn'."

As Katrina awoke, she noticed the sun shining through the window and heard birds singing. She wondered what time it was. She dressed quickly and went into the front room. There were dirty plates on the table, and a fire was going under the stove. She put the pot on the stove after filling it with water. She then pulled out a cup and the tea that Jack had kindly picked up in town the day before. While waiting for the water to get hot, she looked out the window and noticed Uncle Tom and Jack to the side of the barn, fixing the fence. She realized she had slept in. She quickly cleaned up the dishes and then poured some water into her teacup. Just as she sat down to drink her tea, the door opened, and Uncle Tom entered the room.

"Morning, my dear. Hope you slept well," said Uncle Tom.

"Morning, Uncle Tom. I must have slept well since I slept in. I see you have already been working. I meant to be up to help you," replied Katrina.

"I know, honey, but you were tired and needed to get your rest. After you have your cup of tea and breakfast, I will show you around the farm."

Uncle Tom showed some excitement this morning. Katrina thought maybe it was because of her being there. She so wished he hadn't started the process of selling the farm. She wondered if she had a chance to change his mind.

"Uncle Tom, why did you have papers drawn up for the farm?" asked Katrina.

Uncle Tom looked directly at her and responded, "As I said yesterday, I can't afford to keep the farm going. I can't do all the work by myself any more. When your father passed away a couple of years ago, it has gone downhill."

"But why sell it to Jack?" Katrina inquired.

"Because he's been helping on this farm for years and knows the land and the animals. He has been a friend to me. I couldn't have done it without him," stated Tom.

Just then the door opened, and Jack walked in. Katrina turned toward the stove like she wanted to ignore Jack. Tom noticed this. He wondered what was said between the two. He didn't want them to be enemies. *Lord, what can I do to help these two to at least like each other?* thought Tom.

Jack went over to the stove and grabbed the coffee pot and poured a cup then sat in a chair. "Hope I didn't interrupt anything," Jack commented as he sat down.

Katrina looked at Jack then her uncle. She stood up from the table and started to head to the bedroom. Uncle Tom stood up and asked Katrina, "Please don't leave. I want to talk some more."

Katrina stopped then looked directly at Jack. Jack looked at her then at Tom. "I will leave. Sorry to have interrupted," said Jack as he got up and turned to walk out the door.

"No, you stop too, Jack," replied Tom. "I would like you both to sit down. I have some things to say."

Jack looked at Katrina then went to the table and sat across from Tom. Katrina also went to the table and sat next to Uncle Tom. She felt as if her father had just ordered her to do something like she was a child.

Uncle Tom cleared his throat. Katrina jumped up and went to get a cup of coffee for Uncle Tom. She returned the pot to the stove, and as she returned to the table, she looked at Jack and decided to ask him if he wanted one too. She figured she should be civil to him since Uncle Tom asked him to stay for this conversation.

"Would you like one too?" she asked.

Jack looked at her. "I would like one, but I can get my own. Thank you for asking." Jack stood up and got his coffee while Katrina sat down.

Tom waited for Jack to sit down. He took a sip of his coffee and set his cup down.

"Katrina, I am so glad to have you here. If you had come six months ago, I might have been able to keep the farm going, maybe. I am getting old. Jack has been here working beside me for many years as I said before. I thought it was only fair that Jack have the property. Since you have shown up, I have had second thoughts, but realistically I know that you and I can't take care of this farm without help. That is, we can't do it without financial help and manpower. So I was wondering, if you both agree to this, if we can try to keep the farm going, together—the three of us. Jack, this would mean that you will have a personal stake in the farm."

"But what does all this mean for me?" asked Katrina with a trace of jealousy in her voice.

Tom took Katrina's hand and said, "Let's see what you are good at. I would like you to take care of the records. I will have a new batch of calves coming soon and hope that you can help take care of them. Jack will be in the fields doing the planting. Are you willing to give it a try?"

"What about Jack and the agreement you have been working on?" inquired Katrina as she looked from Uncle Tom to Jack and back to Uncle Tom.

"I already spoke to Jack about this, and he has agreed to this plan as long as you do. So what do you say, Katrina?" Uncle Tom let go of her hand and took a sip of his coffee.

Katrina was feeling like she was outnumbered and betrayed. *Uncle Tom already talked to Jack about this. When did they talk? What about the papers that Raymond was working on?* Her mind was racing. Can she give her uncle an honest answer when she wasn't sure? *Might as well be honest.*

"Uncle Tom, I don't know what to say. I need to sort this through my head." Then Katrina hesitated. She looked at both men. "I am not sure what this will really mean for me," cried Katrina as she put her head in her hands. Then the thought crossed her mind that she must gain control. She didn't want to look weak, especially in front of Jack. Katrina pulled herself together and held her head up.

"Katrina, you are sounding like your father. He always was thinkin' things through and analyzing things. Life was short for him. Don't make his mistake. Relax. Take a shot at living your life." Uncle Tom looked at her with sweet eyes that glowed.

Katrina repeated his words in her head. *Uncle Tom was right. She was hesitant at doing things and was always thinking things through. Was it time to take a chance? Should she risk everything and go for what her uncle had asked? She came all this way. What else did she have to do? Where would she go if she didn't stay? Enough!* Katrina knew what she had to do.

"Uncle, you are right. What else would I do or where would I go? I have nowhere else to go. I will stay and help you," Katrina remarked as she tried to smile for Uncle Tom. She sipped her tea to hide her anxiety.

Jack set his coffee cup down and looked at Uncle Tom, wondering what he was thinking about Katrina's conversation. Jack had a feeling that Katrina felt trapped here due to the circumstances. Jack felt a hurt for Katrina. He knew how she was feeling. He wondered what he could do to help her feel comfortable here.

Chapter 5

As the sun climbed high in the sky, Katrina and Uncle Tom rode out behind the barn. As they approached the wood-line, Uncle Tom drew up his horse to a stop and turned in his saddle to look at the pond beyond and then turned back to look at Katrina.

"You know your father cleaned up that pond and cleared the pasture to the right all by himself with his bare hands. His sweat and blood went into it. He was a real hard worker," stated Uncle Tom. "You should have seen him. You would have been proud of him. This farm was his dream."

Katrina rode her horse over toward the pond and stopped by the flowers she noticed her first day on the farm. Uncle Tom rode up beside her. Katrina looked dreamy-eyed at the flowers and said in a voice that sounded just as far away, "I remember Daddy talking about wanting a farm. He said he was going to have all kinds of animals. He would say he was going to have a self-sufficient farm."

After a sob, Katrina couldn't control the tears. She turned away from Uncle Tom so he wouldn't see her crying. She tried to get a hold of herself by taking a deep breath and turned her head toward the field of flowers. As she looked at the gold and yellow swirling colors filling the field, a smile took over her sad facial expression. She knew that this was all a part of God's plan and this was where she needed to be. She wanted to fulfill her father's vision for the farm. With this decision, she turned to Uncle Tom, and with a gasp of breath, she said to him, "I want to finish my father's dream. I am going to make this farm happen, and eventually, it will be self-sufficient." At that moment, she felt a soft wisp of wind, a gentle breeze flow through her hair, brushing against her cheek. She knew then that it was her father acknowledging her wish and showing his agreement to their plan.

The next morning, Katrina woke with a smile, and she felt refreshed and ready to go. She jumped out of bed and got dressed. In the kitchen, she started the coffee for her uncle and put on a pot of hot water for her tea. She grabbed the cast-iron frying pan and put it on the wood stove. Katrina thought about what it would have been like to have served breakfast to her father. He would have loved the eggs and bacon with a steaming hot cup of coffee. He would have loved having her here. As she was in thought, Uncle Tom entered the room and had a shocked look on his face as he saw his niece standing at the stove. He noticed she was smiling and she had a glowing look on her face. He was pleased to see this.

"You look wonderful this morning, Katrina." Her uncle smiled.

"Well, thank you, Uncle Tom. I feel great this morning. I am going to fix you some breakfast first then will you ride with me and show me the rest of the farm? I want to see every inch." Katrina threw bacon in the pan while talking and pulled the eggs out of the icebox. As she took a cup from the one single shelf above the ice box and started to pour the coffee, the door opened as a knock was made at the same time on the outside of the door.

Jack walked in with a burlap bag over his shoulder. He noticed the smiles and felt a peaceful ambience in the room. He liked this feeling and wished he could be a part of it.

"Good morning. Glad to see everyone so happy," Jack chirped.

Uncle Tom looked at the bag that Jack sat down on the floor next to the door then up at Jack. "Wha'cha got in the bag, Jack?"

Jack looked at the bag then at Tom, and he turned toward Katrina. "I was thinking about what we needed to get things started for a garden. It's time to get one in. So I brought some seeds."

"Seeds?" questioned Katrina with a curious look directly at Jack. Uncle Tom laughed and Jack chimed in laughing too.

"I mean, I know what seeds are . . . I was wondering what kind of seeds you brought?" said Katrina as she tried not to laugh but wanted to show a little irritation to hopefully get their goat.

Uncle Tom looked at Jack and stated, "Careful, she's on a roll about getting the farm in shape. You'll need more than seeds." Tom chuckled and took his cup of coffee from Katrina as she leaned across the table to hand the cup to him.

"Would you like a cup of coffee too?" asked Katrina as she went to reach for another cup.

"Yes, I would. And the seeds are ready for planting. Can we start after breakfast?" questioned Jack.

"Sure can, and I have the perfect spot for a garden," replied Katrina, and she smiled while handing him a cup of steaming coffee. As he took the cup, their hands touched, and Katrina felt a warm sensation in her that wasn't from the hot coffee. A tingle went through her that made her shiver slightly. She felt flushed in the face and hoped that Jack and Uncle Tom didn't see the pink color she knew was on her cheeks.

"What are the seeds?" asked Katrina, trying not to not draw attention to herself.

Jack grabbed the bag and put it on a chair next to the table. "There's corn, carrots, potatoes, onion sets, and squash. We can get whatever you want too."

Katrina's eyes grew bigger as he spoke about the different kinds of seeds. "What you have now sounds fantastic! I can't wait to get started." By this time, she had the bacon done and the eggs in the pan. Uncle Tom had the plates out on the table and was getting his second cup of coffee. After he set his coffee mug down, he poured another cup for Jack.

Jack was watching Katrina while she cooked. The smells were sumptuous, and he realized how hungry he was. "Breakfast sure does smell wonderful, doesn't it, Tom?" asked Jack trying to keep the conversation going.

"Thanks," responded Katrina. "It will be ready in just a minute." She poured herself a cup of tea and placed it on the table at her setting. Then she put the bacon on the table and turned to take the eggs off the stove. As she reached for the towel that was on the other side of the stove lying on a stand, her arm touched the handle of the pan on the cast-iron stove. At that very instant, she let out a squeaky soft scream and pulled her arm away from the stove. Jack was up in a flash and grabbed the towel and dipped it quickly in the water pitcher, and as he pulled it out of the pitcher, he wrung the towel of excess water and draped it over Katrina's arm. At the same time, he put his other arm around her and pulled her toward him and embraced her.

As Katrina steadied her feet and felt herself moving, she felt hands supporting her. She looked up and saw Jack's face looking down at her. She didn't feel the pain on her arm anymore. She was focusing on the rugged handsome face looking down at her. She felt like she was going to continue falling to the floor. She felt like she was melting in his arms. She closed her eyes for a brief minute, wondering what she would see if she opened them. As she slowly opened her eyes, she saw his brown eyes looking down at her with warmth and sincerity.

Jack couldn't believe Katrina didn't flinch away from him. He noticed her beautiful face and gorgeous hazel eyes. He thought she looked like an angel, and he was excited to have her in his arms. He wondered if God brought her here to be in his life. He was hoping that was the case.

Uncle Tom cleared his throat to interrupt the moment. He stated, "The day is moving along. Katrina, if you are okay, we need to eat before it gets cold, and then we need to get working on that garden."

This brought both Katrina and Jack out of their hypnotic state of wonderment. Jack released Katrina and moved back to the table then sat down to pick up his fork. He didn't look at either of them. Jack realized that his actions were noticed by Uncle Tom. He felt a little uncomfortable. Katrina put her hand on the cloth that Jack draped on her arm. She reached for another towel and picked up the pan of eggs and moved it to the table then she dished the eggs out to the men and gave herself the little amount that was left. She replaced the pan on the stove and sat down in her seat.

Chapter 6

The garden smelled like fresh dirt and worms as they dug up the ground. The brief rain from the night before made it easy to turn the soil. Katrina kept wiping her brow, and she had dirt streaks on her face and hands. Her hair was falling from her pulled-up bun at the nape of her neck. Jack looked up several times and smiled at the sight of Katrina. Uncle Tom kept looking at the two of them, and he noticed Jack smiling when he was watching Katrina. Tom thought, *Lord, you say all things come in time. I hope so for their sake.*

After a couple of hours working in the garden, Jack went into the barn, and Tom was hitching the horse up to the wagon. Katrina went to the well and returned with a pitcher of water. She went over to Uncle Tom and handed him the pitcher. He took it and gulped down some water then handed it back to her. "Thank you," said Tom, "You are so thoughtful. I certainly needed that." He pulled out his kerchief and wiped his brow. With the wagon hitched and ready to go, Uncle Tom motioned and called for Jack.

Katrina wondered what Uncle Tom was going to do with the wagon. She was still trying to learn the ropes on the farm and didn't understand all the steps to working the fields. She wanted Uncle Tom to teach her all he knew. She had to learn fast so she didn't lose out on this evolving farm that she was starting to fall in love with.

"What are you doing with the wagon, Uncle Tom?" asked Katrina.

"Jack and I are going out to the back pasture to check on the cattle. Remember, I said they would be birthing soon? We need to check on them," replied Uncle Tom.

"But the wagon?" asked a curious Katrina.

"Just in case we have any calves or cows that need help coming back to the barn. Have to be prepared and not waste time on a farm," answered Uncle Tom.

Jack had put the hoe away in the barn and returned to stand by the wagon during Katrina and Tom's conversation. He decided not to interrupt so he could hear what Katrina might have to say.

"Can I go too? I want to help." Katrina was hoping they would let her go. She did say she wanted to learn everything on the farm.

"Sure, climb into the wagon, honey," replied Uncle Tom as he climbed onto the seat of the wagon. Jack reached out to help Katrina climb in the wagon. Katrina was glad he did; as she stepped up, she realized she had some sore muscles from working in the vegetable garden.

Uncle Tom was quiet as they traveled down through the pasture and out behind the woods. Katrina wondered what was on his mind. "Uncle Tom, what are you thinking about?"

Uncle Tom hesitated before answering, "Wondering about the farm and if we can make it go, the three of us. I want this to work for you and for Jack. Then I got to thinking that I'm an old man with just a few years left. What will happen to the farm when I'm gone?"

Katrina thought, *That could be a dilemma.* Then it dawned on her: What will happen? Will Jack want to take it over? Could she financially take it? There's no way they could both keep it . . . Well, there was one way, but she wasn't ready for that, and she didn't know if Jack was the right man for her. She shook her head as if that would help her to stop thinking about the situation and to gather her wits.

Tom noticed Katrina shake her head. "Are you all right?"

Katrina shook her head in a yes motion. As she looked ahead, she noticed some animals. She pointed and at the same time asked her uncle, "Are they ours?" referring to the cattle she saw in the distance.

Uncle Tom strained his eyes and placed his left hand on his forehead to shade the sun from above. "Yup, I do say they are." He drew the wagon up a few yards from the animals and jumped out as if he was in his twenties. He made a moan as he tried to straighten up. Katrina heard the moan, and it reminded her that he really was aging. She went to stand up from the bed of the wagon, and Jack's hands reached up and embraced her waist by wrapping his fingers around the sides of her waist. He lifted her up off the wagon then placed her gracefully down on the ground. Jack let his hands linger around her waist, and he looked into her eyes. Once again, he realized how beautiful she was up close. He wanted to hold her tight and never let go. He felt a stirring in his body that he never felt before.

Katrina felt flushness not only on her face but through her whole body once Jack placed her on the ground. She felt warm and tingly. What an exciting energy rush. It certainly made her feel good. Was this what love was supposed to feel like? Was it love?

Jack released his hold on Katrina, and as he glanced into her eyes, his whole face lit up with a smile. He quickly looked away when she looked up at him. It was then that he noticed Tom bending down to the ground. He had a puzzled look on his face that Katrina noticed, and she heard him say, "Katrina, your uncle!" as he jaunted toward her uncle. She turned to look and saw her uncle's position.

"What is it, Tom?" asked Jack. Jack bent down next to Tom.

As Katrina came up behind them, she tried to look over the top of them, but she couldn't see much. She moved around to the side of Uncle Tom and saw a small bundle. It was a baby calf. Uncle Tom was massaging the body. Tom was clearing the throat with his fingers. "Is it all right?" asked Katrina.

Jack was the first to respond, "As long as we get him cleaned up and wrap him. Please get a blanket from the wagon and hurry back."

Katrina ran to the wagon and found a gray flannel blanket and ran back to the men. As she handed Jack the blanket, she noticed the calf was breathing heavy. "What can I do to help?" she asked.

Jack asked her to hold the blanket down as the calf started to kick. Katrina did just that and started talking softly to the calf. "It's okay, boy. You're going to be fine. You're in very good hands." Katrina started to rub the blanket against the body of the little animal. She took her other hand and put it on the head, softly caressing the calf's head and still talking to it. "You're a cutie. God certainly blessed you as you're a big boy." Katrina looked around. "Where's your mama?"

During this time, Uncle Tom had gotten up and had gone over to a bigger body about a couple of yards away. He stood looking at the mound. Jack saw that the calf was in good hands with Katrina, and he followed Tom to the other animal. Tom shook his head and said to Jack, "Looks like she didn't make it. We'll have to butcher her here and carry the meat back."

Jack remarked, "And we'll take the baby back to the barn. Katrina now has her first farm chore." Jack looked back at Katrina who was watching the men and listening. After Jack spoke, she looked down at the calf and bent over to caress him and gave him a hug. *Poor baby*, she thought. Jack came over and picked the calf up and carried him over to the wagon. He placed him near the back of the seat then turned to Katrina. "Will you sit with him while your uncle and I take care of the mother?"

"I'd be glad to. What do I do?" inquired Katrina.

Jack had started to walk over to Tom by the mound and turned his head to talk to Katrina. "Just keep him warm and down. I will bring you some milk for him shortly." He turned back toward Tom. When he reached Tom, he went down on his knees and pulled his knife out. In just a short time. they had the meat cut up and loaded on the wagon in burlap bags. The calf was lying still next to Katrina. She had kept the blanket around the newborn.

The sun was high overhead as they reached the barn. Uncle Tom was the first to climb down from the wagon once it stopped. He grabbed one of the sacks of meat and took it to the root cellar. Jack followed in Tom's actions. After four trips each, the meat was all taken care of. Jack approached the wagon to see Katrina still sitting with the calf.

"Sorry, Katrina. We had to get the meat where it was cold before it turned. You can move down so I can help you get off the wagon." Katrina automatically slid down the wagon bed and faced Jack as he lifted her from the edge and set her down on the ground. Katrina brushed her dress off and noticed Jack hadn't stepped away. She looked up at Jack. "I just want to say you did a wonderful job with that little one. Thank you."

"My pleasure," replied Katrina. She turned to look at the animal she just cared for.

Chapter 7

Katrina headed to the barn. It had become routine to wake up and get dressed for the barn. He had grown quite a bit in the past couple of weeks. Katrina learned how to feed him and water him, and she spent time playing with him. She wanted to name him but couldn't come up with an appropriate name. She kept calling him Babes, and he responded to her calls. When she walked into the barn, he was now running up to her. He would follow her all over.

Jack came every day to work the fields and help Uncle Tom with the animals. He would join them for breakfast and supper. It was becoming routine for him, and he liked the daily pattern. But he felt like he was missing something lately. He tried to think about it and to figure out what the void was he felt in his life. He knew someday he would want to get married. He was pulled out of his reverie when he heard a horse ride up.

Raymond dismounted from his horse and walked over to where Jack was working in the garden that was sprouting greens all over. He reached his hand out toward Jack to shake hands. "Morning! Is Tom Martin around? I'm Mr. Raymond Coats. Remember me?"

Jack shook his head yes. As he looked to the barn, the door opened, and Tom walked through the doors. He noticed the man standing next to Jack, and it dawned on him who the gentleman was. He walked over to the garden and up to the man standing next to Jack. Tom shook hands with him and said, "I remember you, Mr. Coats. What can I do for you?"

Tom's submissiveness puzzled Raymond. "I have the paperwork completed that we talked about the last time I was here."

Katrina was coming from the barn when she heard the gentleman talk. She stopped short in her tracks and felt the wind being knocked out of her. Her mind started to race with thoughts. *Oh no, everything has been going well and now he is here. This day . . . What's going to happen?* She started to shake. She saw the men walk toward the house. She tried to move and felt she couldn't take one step in any direction. She took a deep breath and looked up to the sky. *Lord, help me to understand what is to be. I need to move to the house. Please guide me in that direction. Give me the strength to encounter the situation, and I pray this comes out for the best. You know, Lord, in my heart that I want to stay here. I am not sure how I feel about Jack, but I don't want to leave nor lose this farm. It is Uncle Tom's life, and I hope he sees that since I have come here, there has been a big change. Please guide us, Lord.* Her feet moved, and she hurriedly headed toward the house entering the side door.

Katrina headed inside and went to the stove to make coffee. While the pot of coffee was perking, she pulled out some cookies and placed them on the table. The men entered the room and sat down. Mr. Coats reached for a piece of paper from his satchel. She saw Mr. Coats hand the paper to Jack. She looked up at Jack's face and then looked at Uncle Tom. Uncle Tom had a look of discernment. A twinge of pain shot through Katrina's stomach. She sat down and clutched the table edge. Jack happened to see Katrina's movement, and he felt a twinge in his heart for Katrina's pain that he knew she was enduring. Jack took the paper in his hands and held it up. Uncle Tom looked at Jack and said, "Wait, Jack. I want to say something." Jack put the paper down to let Tom talk. He looked again at Katrina. She had a ghostly white look on her face.

Uncle Tom took the paper in his hands and looked at Katrina. "I have this paper that was drawn up before my niece came here. She has proven to me that she wants to be a part of this farm. I can't run this farm by myself. Katrina has been helpful, but she can't run this farm without help."

Raymond now had a puzzled look on his face. Jack began to wonder what Tom was up to. Was he going through with the original contract of having Jack buy him out with the option to stay on the farm for life? Jack wasn't sure that he wanted to go through with the contract. He knew he needed to help with the farm. He knew he had special feelings for Katrina, but he also knew he would be pushing her away if it was to go through. Jack had to speak up now. He realized he didn't want Katrina to go away.

"Tom, I would like to take the contract and tear it up. I don't want to take this place away from you and Katrina," stated Jack.

Katrina quickly looked at Jack. She was extremely surprised to hear Jack make his offer. She showed a look of surprise and puzzlement. *Why was Jack doing this? He wanted the farm. He's put a lot of time and sweat into this farm.* She wondered if he and Uncle Tom had talked. That didn't make sense since Uncle Tom had talked several times about getting older and not being able to take care of the farm.

Uncle Tom piped up, "I have it all figured out." He turned to Mr. Coats and handed him the document. "I want to make some changes to this document." Both Katrina and Jack quickly looked at Mr. Coats, wondering what his take was on making changes.

Raymond took the document and opened it up. He searched through the document and opened to a specific page. "Okay, what are your changes?" he asked as he put his pen in his hand.

Uncle Tom looked at Katrina and then at Jack and back to Katrina. "I wanted to talk to you both about this, but Mr. Coats returned sooner than I expected. Katrina, now that you are here, I want to include you in the ownership of the farm. My original agreement with Jack is that he was to take over ownership of the farm with my having lifetime use. I now want to keep that the same . . ."

Katrina's heart sank, and her stomach went into knots. She must have had an awful look on her face when she realized Jack had moved next to her and Uncle Tom had gotten up. He brought her a glass of water.

"I don't mean to make you upset, my dear. Please let me finish," exclaimed Uncle Tom. "I want you and Jack to have the farm. I want to put the contract in both your names. I hope this is acceptable by both of you.

Katrina looked at Jack, wondering how he felt about this. Jack took her hand and held it in his hand. "Katrina, I am okay with this change. It is your uncle's farm, and if this is what he wants, then I will be pleased to share the farm with you. You have shown a genuine interest in the farm. You have a vested interest and family connection with this farm. I am not about to take that away from you. I hope that you will agree to let me continue helping with the farm. There is too much for one person to do. What do you say, Katrina?" Jack was almost holding his breath waiting for her answer.

There was silence for about thirty seconds before Katrina said anything. Uncle Tom thought she was going to not accept the contract. He was sure she was going to want the farm to herself. Then it dawned on him that she had sent a telegram a while back. Maybe she was waiting for a response. He started fidgeting with his hands then wringing them. Jack noticed Tom's nervousness and wondered if Katrina saw it.

Katrina cleared her throat then said, "I came here expecting to help you, Uncle Tom, with this farm. I left a life back east. I don't want to go back. I want to be here with you and where my father grew up and be a part of family. I see that right now it takes all three of us to work the farm. If Jack is willing to help on the farm . . . I know I can't do it by myself." She took a long pause then responded, "I am willing to accept the contract."

Uncle Tom let out a sigh of relief with a grin. Katrina saw that he was pleased with her decision. Jack was still holding her hand. Her hand felt nice and warm, but she realized Jack's hand become clammy. He was sweating, which meant he was worried. Katrina squeezed his hand that was holding her hands. Jack was surprised and squeezed back his acknowledgment. This made Katrina release a soft smile. Tom saw this exchange of emotion between Katrina and Jack. He knew then that everything was going to work out, and he sank back into his chair and thanked God then turned to Mr. Coats. "Please make the changes, and then we will sign the document."

Mr. Coats started writing on the paper. In the meantime, Katrina released her hands from Jack's grip. She pulled her chair back and stood up. Jack was hoping she wasn't upset. He still wasn't sure how to read her emotions. He wondered, *Is she going to change her mind?* Jack was getting nervous again. He thought, *Why am I think-*

ing like this? Everything is going to be all right. Right, Jesus? I need her in my life. Please help me to keep her here and for her to be willing to want me in her life. Thank you, Lord.

Katrina got up and grabbed the coffee pot and started pouring coffee into all the cups. She replaced the pot on the stove and got herself a cup of tea water and sat back down with a smile on her face.

Uncle Tom thanked Jesus Christ for letting this happen so easily and peacefully. He now knew that if anything should happen to him, the farm would continue and still be with family. This pleased him.

Mr. Coats finished the changes and handed the document back to Tom. He read the contract then said, "This works for me." He handed the contract to Jack and Katrina. "What do you think?" They both read it, and Katrina nodded her head. Tom handed Jack the pen. Jack turned the pen over to Katrina, and she took the pen and asked Mr. Coats where she was to sign. Raymond pointed to the spot after turning the page. After signing, Katrina turned the paper to Jack. He took the pen and paper and signed below Katrina's signature then handed the papers to Tom. After Tom signed, he handed the papers back to Raymond. "How much do I owe you for this transaction?" asked Tom.

Raymond responded, "Twenty dollars."

Katrina noticed Jack reach into his pocket and pull out money and then count out and hand paper money to Mr. Coats. Jack commented, "Here's the payment in full. When will we have the final contract?"

Raymond said, "Once I get it to the office and have it marked and returned, I would say about two months."

Chapter 8

The next day, Katrina was in the barn taking care of the calves. It was difficult to believe that there were so many calves already. Uncle Tom was right when he said that once they start birthing, there would be a fair number of calves to take care of. She went from one to the next until she had fed all of them. She loved taking care of these precious creatures from God. They each had their own personality. She wanted to name each one but soon realized that it would be complicated to do so. She wondered how she would be able to recognize each one and connect a name with each of them.

After feeding and watering the calves, Katrina went into the house to get a drink. She decided to take a pitcher of water to the men in the field. Just as she gathered some cookies and the pitcher and started walking out the door, she heard horses approaching. As she looked up, she noticed Mr. Whitaker on one of the horses. There were several other men on the other horses. As they rode up to the house, Mr. Whitaker recognized Katrina and dismounted from his horse. He walked up to her. She put the items down on the table located next to a rocker and turned toward him. "Mr. Whitaker, what a surprise."

Mr. Whitaker reached out his hand and took her right hand into his. "My pleasure, Miss . . . I don't remember your given name. Katrina, I believe?"

"Yes, Katrina Martin."

"Miss Martin—"

"You can call me Katrina, sir."

"I need to talk to Jack. Can you tell me where he is?" inquired Mr. Whitaker.

"He's out in the field with my uncle. I was just heading out there."

"May I walk out with you, Katrina? It is urgent that I see him."

"Of course," Katrina turned to gather the pitcher and basket.

Mr. Whitaker turned to talk to the men he had with him. Katrina noticed the men dismount and stand by their horses as Mr. Whitaker walked back up to her, took the pitcher from her, and embraced her elbow with his other hand and guided her past the barn. "Which field are they in?" he asked.

As Katrina and Mr. Whitaker approached the field where Jack and Tom were, Jack noticed them and stopped working. Tom noticed Jack stop and look toward the pasture. Tom then noticed Albert Whitaker. Albert was a man with a vision and a purpose. Tom knew Albert for as long as he lived on the farm, which was since they were boys. He recalled Albert walking to school with him when they weren't busy in the fields with their fathers. Albert's family had money and could make the family farm grow and be successful. The Whitaker farm had thousands of acres and numerous animals from cattle to horses, to hogs and chickens. Tom knew that Albert was a man who worked hard and had everything he wanted. Tom wondered what brought him to this little farm. Albert didn't go anywhere without a reason.

Jack pulled out his kerchief and wiped his face from the dripping sweat and walked toward Katrina and Mr. Whitaker. As he reached them, he took the pitcher from Mr. Whitaker and took a swig of water. By that time, Tom had walked over, and Jack handed him the pitcher to drink from. Jack shook hands with Mr. Whitaker. Tom followed with the hand shaking and greeted Albert like they had just met.

"Hello, Mr. Whitaker. What brings you here?"

Albert Whitaker was a man with few words as he responded, "I need to talk to you and Jack. Could we go back to the house?"

Jack was the first to respond. "Sure. We can finish this later." He turned to Tom and took the hoe from him and went to put it in the wagon. Jack climbed in the wagon after helping Tom and Katrina up on the back of the wagon. As Jack looked at Albert, he pointed to the seat beside him, and Albert climbed up with ease. Jack urged the horses to move, and they rode back to the house in silence.

Once they approached the house, everyone climbed out of the wagon and went inside. Katrina asked if anyone wanted a cup of coffee or water. Albert responded first. "I would like some water please." He sat at the table next to Tom. Everyone else also asked for water since it was such a warm day. After pouring water into the glasses and serving the men, Katrina sat down.

Tom was the first to speak as he noticed Albert was hesitating and having trouble finding the words for what he wanted to say. Albert's hesitation puzzled Jack as this was very unusual for Mr. Whitaker as he was usually a man who spoke his mind.

"What's on your mind, Albert?" questioned Tom.

"I took Mrs. Whitaker to the doctor's this morning. She has not been feeling well. The doctor says she doesn't have long to live. She has some sort of arthritic pain inside that he can't take care of. I had my lawyer do some research, and we heard of a place in New York State that can help folks who are suffering like that. There is a sulfur-fed spring there that has miraculous healing powers. I plan to take Hilda there to see if there is help for her. I figure we will be gone for as long as it takes. My foreman will be running the ranch . . . but I need someone to help look after things for me."

Albert turned to Tom. "Tom, we have been friends for many years. I know you have the skills to run my ranch like you used to do a long time ago. I hate to ask this, but will you take over for me while I am away?" As Albert was talking, he was wringing his hands and held a very concerned look on his face. It was almost like he was on the edge of tears. Jack noticed this and started to become emotional himself. He looked up to Mr. Whitaker. This was a man with compassion yet full of sternness and determination.

Tom looked at Katrina then Jack and then at Albert. "I will have to ask Katrina and Jack if that is possible. They are doing well with running this farm, and the question is, can they do without me? Albert, it's been a long time since I have been in control of a place like yours. As you can see my farm didn't amount to much." Tom had a concerned look on his face, and he wondered what Katrina would say. Would it be fair to her to leave her here and alone with Jack? Not that he had anything to worry about there since Jack stayed at his place during the night, but then that would leave Katrina here by herself at night. Tom then wondered if he would be able to go back and forth during the daytime and be with Katrina at night so she wouldn't be alone.

"Albert, there's a few things to work out for this to happen . . ."

Albert interrupted Tom. "Name it. Whatever you need or want, it's yours. Tom, we have had our differences in the past, and I have forgiven you for all the things that you have done and I hope you have forgiven me for my shenanigans. Hilda is my world. I need to do what I can for her. If that means leaving the ranch to find help for her, then that is what I must do. Tom, I need your help more than ever now. I would ask Jack to do this, but I know you need his help here too. In fact, if you need help with the ranch, have Jack help you, and you can send some men here to work your fields. That is actually a great idea and might make things easier for you."

Albert turned to Jack. "Would you mind helping Tom with the ranch? I trust both of you and know you can take care of everything. Then you can have some men work here so that things get done around here too. That would help Katrina too so she ain't having to work so hard." Albert turned directly at each of them with a pleading look.

Katrina was now the first to say anything. "Uncle Tom, this decision is for you and Jack. This is your farm."

"Now remember the contract, Katrina. It is as much yours as it is mine and Jack's, so you have as much of a say in this."

Jack wondered what Tom really wanted to do. He knew he would follow Tom in whatever decision he made. "Tom, I will do whatever you want me to do."

Albert looked straight at Tom and said, "It looks like the decision is yours. I will respect what you want to do. Just know that I will make this worth your while in the long run."

Albert became concerned when there was no immediate response from Tom. He was starting to become frantic. "Tom, if I have to, I will leave the ranch as is, and God knows what will happen. To be honest with you, I don't trust my foreman. I need someone there that I can trust. I am desperate to leave, and I must go soon as time is not on Hilda's side, and the trip will take a while as it is. Please?"

Tom stood up from the table and started to pace to the door and back. There was complete silence as Tom did some mulling over in his head as to whether to accept or not. This was an opportunity that he had always dreamed of. When he was helping with the Whitaker ranch in the past, he was very happy. But at that time, Katrina's father was keeping the family farm, and his health was failing. He had more of a commitment to his brother then and had to leave the ranch to help his brother. Now here was that opportunity once again. Some fellows never got a second chance. Katrina and Jack could run this place and with being able to send some help here, the farm could get ahead. That would be a great help to Katrina when she takes it over. He decided he had to do this. If nothing else, this was the opportunity to help Katrina get a head start with the farm.

"Albert"—Tom turned back toward the table and looked directly at Mr. Whitaker—"I accept your request. But I would like to have it in writing that you are giving me permission to run your ranch during your absence and that I can do things as I see fit. That way, your foreman can't do anything to take control. Agreed?"

"Agreed," exclaimed Albert as he stood to shake Tom's hand. "You are a smart businessman. I knew it all along. Thank you so much!"

Katrina looked at Jack to see what his expression was from this decision. She noticed Jack was smiling. Now she was puzzled, wondering why Jack was smiling. What was he thinking? Katrina wondered if this change would be too much for Uncle Tom. Then she had a thought: What if something happened to Uncle Tom while he was running the Whitaker place? That should be decided now too. "I have one question. What happens if something should occur to Uncle Tom?"

"Jack will take over then," replied Albert with no hesitation as if that wasn't even a question. "I will go into town now and have the paperwork drawn up. Jack, I would like for you to go with me. I have some other things we need to talk about." Albert turned to Tom. "As soon as the paperwork is done, hopefully by tomorrow, I will have someone stop by for your signature."

Albert walked over to Tom, who was now standing by the window looking out over the fields that were in plain sight and put his hand on Tom's shoulder. "Thank you, my friend. I know we haven't had much to say these past years, but you don't know what this really means to me."

Tom turned to Albert and while they were still shaking hands, Tom reached his other arm to Albert's shoulder, pulling him forward to give him a hug. "Yes, my friend, I do. And thank you for thinking that I can do this. That means a lot to me."

Jack walked over and shook Tom's hand then Albert's hand and proceeded out the door to the barn. Albert turned to Katrina and tipped his head as a gesture of thanks and walked out of the house. Katrina walked over to Uncle Tom and embraced him. "Uncle Tom, I am proud of you as I am sure this was a very difficult decision. Just tell me what I need to do, and I will do everything I can for you."

Tom watched Albert and Jack ride away as he walked out toward the barn. Tom had some things to do before he could go manage the Whitaker ranch. He entered the barn and proceeded to the loft, climbing up the ladder and crawling to the back corner where he wiped away some loose straw to bare a wooden chest that was about the size of a bureau. As he managed to pull the chest out, scraping it along the floor and moving it side to side to place it where he could open the top, he remembered how he first met Katrina's mother at a dance. He and Katrina's father, Matt who was his younger brother, were there at the dance. Katrina's mother was young and beautiful. Both Matt and Tom instantly liked her as they took turns dancing with her that night. Matt ended up the one she liked, and Tom stepped back because Albert had offered him the position of manager and he wanted to make sure he had a future before taking a wife. He thought that he would have to let Katrina know how her mom and dad met.

Tom fumbled through the items in the box and pulled out a leather hat. He brushed it off and put it on his head. It seemed to still fit but needed a good cleaning. Tom repacked everything back in the trunk except the hat. He closed the trunk and pushed it back in the corner and threw some straw on top of it. As he was climbing back down the ladder, he heard the door open; and just as he reached the barn floor, he turned and saw Katrina entering the barn.

"Uncle Tom, what are you doing?" questioned Katrina as she noticed the hat on his head. Then she gave a chuckle.

Uncle Tom took the hat off and looked at it. It looked worn. His hat was light brown with dark streaked stains and a torn leather strip around the band. He then replaced it on his head. He also chuckled and responded to Katrina, "Like it? It's the hat I used to wear when I was the foreman at the Whitaker ranch. Does it look funny?"

"No, but it looks like it could use a cleaning." Katrina winked.

"That it does," remarked Uncle Tom as he took it off once again and turned over the hat, inspecting it.

Katrina was surprised that Uncle Tom was so quick to find his hat. He must be excited to do this new job. She did notice the sparkle in his eyes during the engaged conversation with Tom and Jack. *This might be just the thing for him*, she thought.

As evening drew near, Katrina had supper on the table when Uncle Tom entered the room. Uncle Tom was washing up when the door opened and Jack walked in. Katrina reached for another plate and cup then set them on the table with silverware. As they sat, Jack asked if he could say the blessing. Katrina glanced up quickly at Jack, surprised at what he asked. She automatically put her hands in prayer position and noticed Uncle Tom doing the same.

Jack bowed his head and prayed, "Dear, Lord. Thank you for the new opportunities offered to Tom, Katrina, and myself. I hope that we can meet your expectations. We also pray that Mr. and Mrs. Whitaker have a safe trip and that the sulfur springs help to heal her. Please look on us as we accept the work that has been bestowed upon us. Thank you for your presence, Lord. Amen."

Katrina couldn't believe her ears. She didn't know Jack was religious. He never showed that side before. And she wondered what brought this around. Then it struck her that she hadn't been very religious since she had arrived at Widow's Peak. What happened? Why didn't she go to church? Was there a reason? She felt ashamed and said a quiet prayer, *Lord, please forgive me for not going to church. I'm not sure what came over me. I know better. I promise to go to church from now on. Thank you, Lord.*

The papers were delivered two days later by a young boy from town. Jack was just heading out to the barn when the boy arrived, so he accepted the papers. He turned around and went back into the house. Tom was still at the table, and Jack handed him the papers then sat next to him. Jack called for Katrina, who was in the next room. Katrina quickly came out of her bedroom and sat on the other side of Uncle Tom. "That didn't take long."

Uncle Tom had already opened the papers and started reading. He showed no facial expression while he read. Then he put the papers down and started to get up. Katrina looked at Uncle Tom then at Jack. Jack looked at Tom and questioned, "Well?" Jack was starting to worry.

Katrina noticed Jack wrinkle up his forehead. She saw that look one other time, so she knew it was a worried look. That look happened when Albert Whitaker told them about his wife and her medical condition. She couldn't stand the suspense any longer. "Well? What does it say? Is it what you expected?"

Uncle Tom sat back down in his chair and pulled the paper toward him. As he tapped the paper, he looked at Katrina. "This is perfect. I couldn't have said it better myself. Albert put in everything we talked about and some things we didn't talk about. This contract is very fair and just."

Jack blew out his breath as a sign of relief. "That is wonderful!"

Tom knew that he had to sign the contract but also knew he had to keep Jack and Katrina involved. "Jack, Katrina, I want you to read this over too. If you find anything that needs to change or you have anything to add, now's the time."

Katrina didn't really know what she wanted in this contract. She figured if Uncle Tom and Jack accepted it then she would too. She took the papers and moved them in front of Jack. "Jack, you should read them next. You are more familiar with what is needed in a contract. What do you think?"

Jack looked up at Katrina with a smile and then asked her if she would get him a cup of coffee while he read the papers. He then pulled the lamp closer to have better light and started reading the papers. Katrina retrieved a cup from the shelf and poured coffee into it and set it next to Jack's arm. Jack reached for it with his other hand as Katrina was setting it down. His hand rested on her hand that was still holding the cup. At that same moment, Jack looked up into Katrina's eyes and noticed how blue they were today and that she had beautiful long lashes. Katrina started to pull her hand away. Jack left his hand on top as Katrina looked back into his eyes. Katrina saw dreamy, brown eyes that were staring back at her. She looked away and felt her cheeks blush. Jack still had his hand on top of her hand. Her hands felt warm and soft. Jack wanted to take her in his arms and hold her. But Jack figured it still was too soon to make the move. He didn't want to upset her. He wasn't quite sure how she would react toward him. Was she ready to really like him? She wasn't mad at him like she was when they first met. Jack pulled his hand away to let Katrina move her hand away.

Katrina quickly moved back to the stove with the coffee pot and kept her back turned away from Jack's view. She felt tingly all over. His touch was warm and soft. She wondered what it would be like to be in his arms. Would that ever be possible? They didn't get along in the beginning. Would it ever be possible for them to have something special between the two of them? She knew she had a special feeling for Jack.

In the meantime, Uncle Tom noticed what was going on between Katrina and Jack. He had the biggest grin on his face. He decided to leave them alone so he stood up and went outside. He saw that they didn't notice him leave the room.

Jack went back to reading the papers after sipping some coffee. He didn't look up at Katrina as he didn't want to embarrass her. Katrina set the pot down and walked over to stoke the fire in the fireplace. She turned slightly to see that Jack was still reading the papers. She didn't want to disturb him anymore so she decided to go outside and check on the garden. As she stepped outside and off the porch she felt a gust of air—a warm breeze that tugged gently at her hair and dress. The breeze felt wonderful, and Katrina remembered what her father said one time about how the wind could tell a person what was happening. Her father said a gentle breeze—a gust of wind, as he called it—meant that everything was good and that it was a sign that God was watching over a person. Katrina felt good at that moment. She felt content and happy.

Chapter 9

After breakfast, Katrina was cleaning up the dishes when she heard a rider coming up the path. Uncle Tom stepped out onto the porch to see who it was and what they wanted. The rider was a young boy. She recalled seeing him in town then remembered he was the errand boy. The boy dismounted from his horse, and as he walked up to Uncle Tom, he handed him an envelope. Katrina noticed they were conversing as she stepped out on the porch, wiping her hands on her apron as she took it off.

The boy looked over at Katrina and pointed to her while holding another envelope. Uncle Tom looked at Katrina and motioned for her to come over to where he was standing. Katrina didn't hesitate and walked up to Uncle Tom as the boy handed her the envelope he had in his hand. Then the boy turned away from them and mounted his horse and rode away.

Uncle Tom was the first to speak. "These"—he held up the papers—"are the final contracts. Everything is official now for my running the Whitaker ranch and what involves you and Jack with the Martin farm. I pray that we all do the job we have been given and to know that we are blessed with what God has given us."

Katrina now knew that it did please Uncle Tom to be handling the Whitaker ranch. She noticed how excited and happy he looked when he was holding up the contract. Now she hoped that she would be happy. She still worried about how things were going to shape up with the Martin farm and with Jack and her both owning and running it. Is this what God wanted for her? Why did he bring her here, knowing all the changes that were going to happen here? Katrina was confused. She still was hesitant about Jack. Even though she felt something strange when she was around him, she wasn't sure this was the right thing. These past couple of weeks, she had settled in and was going along with all that has been happening. Now she began to wonder if she had been coasting along and if that was the best thing. During this thinking, Katrina suddenly realized that she hadn't heard anything from the message she sent back home. Not home, but back in Pennsylvania. She held the envelope in her hand and looked at it. She held it up and thought, *Maybe this is my response.*

Katrina went inside and to her room. As she closed the door, she started to open the envelope then went to sit on the side of her bed. She unfolded the paper and started to read to herself.

> *Dear Miss Martin,*
>
> *I am pleased to hear that you arrived safely to your uncle's farm. I continue to investigate the circumstances to your dilemma and currently cannot give you any further acknowledgement to the resolution of this case. I have several contacts still exploring the claim and searching for the perpetrators.*
>
> *I will send a post once I have resolved the case. If you should have any additional information that you believe will assist us to bring this to a closure, please let me know.*
>
> *In the meantime, please know that I hope that this move you have made will give you peace of mind and contentment.*
>
> *Sincerely yours,*
> *Ronald Taylor, Esquire*

Katrina wondered what was taking them so long with the case. She was becoming agitated and knew she had to know more. It was time to send another telegraph. She realized she hadn't been to town in a while and wanted to check out the church and pick up some things at the general store. She decided she was going into town tomorrow.

Katrina went to the barn to take care of the calves and do her routine chores. She wanted to keep herself busy, and she preferred to not be around Jack and maybe she would stay clear of Uncle Tom until supper. After she finished her barn chores, she went into the garden and picked vegetables that were waiting to go on the table. With a basket full of vegetables, Katrina headed toward the house. It was almost time to fix supper. As she entered the front room, she saw Uncle Tom sitting in his chair. She was surprised since he never came in this early, least of all sitting down at this time of day. She panicked at the thought that he might not feel well. She immediately went over to his side and squatted near him. He looked directly at her as she inquired to his well-being. Uncle Tom just sat there and stared at her.

"Uncle Tom, please tell me what is the matter," begged Katrina as she reached over and touched his arm.

Uncle Tom then took his other hand and put it over her hand that she had placed on his arm as he said, "Jack was at the Whitaker Ranch earlier today, and when he returned, he informed me that Mrs. Whitaker never made it out of the house. Albert and Hilda were to leave tomorrow for their trip to the sulfur springs, but she died this morning."

"Oh, Uncle Tom, I am so sorry to hear this. We will have to pay our respects. What is the tradition of doing that out here?" inquired Katrina.

Just then Jack walked in. Uncle Tom stood up and asked Jack how things were. Uncle Tom sounded real sincere and so sad. She didn't understand why Uncle Tom was so touched by this situation. She wondered why he took this so hard. Did he know the Whitakers that well?

Jack responded, "The service will be held the day after tomorrow at the ranch. Tom, we will be needing some help with some of the arrangements. Can you?" Tom shook his head yes. Jack looked at Katrina and asked her for her help too. "Katrina, we will need your help also. Mr. Whitaker is beside himself with the loss of his wife, and the young ones will need assistance in getting ready for the funeral. Mr. Whitaker was wondering if you can help."

Katrina stood up and was very surprised to be asked such a question. She didn't know any of them, why her? Just then she remembered Mrs. Beechwood. "What about Mrs. Beechwood?"

Jack replied, "Didn't you know she went back east last week?"

"No, I didn't," Katrina responded in an apologetic voice.

"Those young ones don't have a mother figure now. They will need help from a woman. You're the only one around without going into town. Mr. Whitaker doesn't trust just anyone with his children. He asked for you."

"He did?" remarked a very surprised Katrina. Why would Mr. Whitaker want her to help with his children? They didn't know her. One would think that there was someone else around or some family member they could bring in. She then thought it would take time to bring someone in and they needed someone now. This would be a temporary position. That wouldn't be a problem. This situation would mean that she would have to postpone her trip to town. But that would only be temporary too. "I can help until they get family in to help."

Jack was surprised to hear her response. He wondered what she meant. Didn't she want to look after the children? What was she afraid of? He knew he couldn't worry about that now; it was important that Johnny and Lizzy had someone to look after them in the meantime. "You may want to get some clothes together, and I will take you to the ranch before sunset."

"What about supper?" questioned Katrina.

"We will get supper at the ranch," remarked Jack with a matter-of-fact voice.

"I don't want to intrude on the family at a time like this," responded Katrina. She wondered what was wrong with this man inviting them to supper at a time when the family was grieving. *How uncompassionate he must be*, she thought.

Jack was bewildered at Katrina's remarks. He figured she must have come from a place that was cruel and rude. How could someone think the way she did in a time like this when a person should be reaching out and helping in every way they can? He then thought that maybe she just wasn't brought up to assist others. The Whitakers had a cook and house servants.

"I believe you forget that there's a cook who will continue to fix meals. It won't be an imposition to them. And your job will be to spend time with Johnny and Lizzy to help them get through the next few days. Remember, they have lost their mother!" Jack made this statement with an undertone of disgust. He couldn't believe she would be so insensitive.

Katrina was confused and hurt. She didn't mean to sound unforgiving. She felt hurt by Jack's response. And then she realized that he meant well and he was asking—no, Mr. Whitaker was asking for her assistance. "Jack, I will help. I am sorry if I sounded so inconsequential. I didn't mean to be that way. I am just surprised to be asked to help a man who could hire someone . . ." Suddenly it hit Katrina. Was he planning on hiring her? "I don't want him to pay me. Please don't get me wrong. I would be pleased to help. I will go gather some clothes now." Katrina left the room and went into her bedroom.

Boy, did I put my foot in my mouth. Why was I so mixed up during that conversation with Jack? I just can't believe that I have been asked to take care of two children who live in a house with all kinds of servants. But how selfish could she be. These two little ones just lost their mother. They will need someone who can be there for them. She might as well be there as here on the farm. Maybe staying there and helping would give her time to sort things out in her head.

As Katrina walked into the huge white house, she saw flowers on the center table and heard a lot of commotion in the room to the right. She looked in and noticed a coffin on a table and chairs being placed around the room by several men. She also saw several floral arrangements that stood on the floor and took up a lot of space in the room. She wondered how they got such large bouquets and so quickly.

She heard a sobbing sound up the stairs. She looked up and saw a small shape sitting at the back corner of the landing near the first doorway. Katrina walked up the stairs toward the small person crouched down with her legs tucked under her arms. It was Lizzy. Katrina bent down and sat next to her on the floor. She put her arms around the little one, and Lizzy looked up at Katrina then nestled her face into Katrina's shoulder and sobbed her heart out. Katrina sat there with Lizzy in her arms and brushed her hand over Lizzy's hair. They sat there for a while without a word between them. Lizzy stopped crying and just leaned against Katrina. Katrina didn't know what to say.

Suddenly, Lizzy looked up at Katrina and said, "Thank you. I miss Mommy already and didn't want to cry in front of Daddy." There was a pause and a sob from Lizzy then she added, "I don't know where Johnny is. He took off a while ago. I hope Jack finds him. Johnny won't say that he will miss Mommy."

Katrina cupped Lizzy's head and pulled her close to her chest and with sincerity whispered to Lizzy, "You will be fine. Johnny will be too. Remember you still have your father and each other."

Lizzy remarked in a soft voice, "And Jack."

Katrina was taken back. Why would Lizzy say Jack at a time like this? Katrina repeated questioningly, "And Jack?"

"Jack is my big brother."

"His mommy died, and then daddy married my mommy. I love Jack so much. He helps around here a lot."

Katrina now understood how much Jack meant to this ranch. It made sense now. Jack wanted to buy the Martin Farm to expand the Whitaker ranch. This started to get Katrina's feathers ruffled, and Lizzy looked up while Katrina was quiet.

"You like Jack, don't you?"

Katrina didn't know what to say. She didn't want to say anything bad about Jack to his sister, especially now. She responded to Lizzy, "He's a friend who helps my uncle." There, that should be enough.

Lizzy stood up and said she felt better and thanked Katrina for being there. Lizzy went down stairs. Katrina sat there for a few minutes mulling over what was taking place and whether she should be there or not.

The main door to the house opened and closed with a loud slamming sound. Katrina stood up and brushed off her dress and headed down the stairs. Mr. Whitaker walked across the foyer and went down the hall toward the dining room. He never saw Katrina. Then Katrina heard sounds down the hall as she walked through the foyer. She heard voices.

"I have made the announcement in town. Folks should be arriving about ten o'clock tomorrow." Katrina knew that was Jack's voice.

Then she heard Mr. Whitaker say, "Okay. Have you seen the little ones?"

Jack responded that he found Johnny out by the creek a while ago. He said Johnny was crying then he watched Johnny go to the horse barn and into the stall with his pony. Jack said he figured he would leave Johnny to himself for a while to do his grieving.

"What about Lizzy?" inquired Mr. Whitaker.

Katrina walked in at that time and informed Mr. Whitaker that Lizzy had a good cry and was somewhere around. Suddenly, Lizzy bounded into the room and ran up to her daddy with her arms wide open. Mr. Whitaker opened his arms and picked Lizzy up and hugged her tight. "Daddy, is Mommy already in heaven?"

Mr. Whitaker swallowed hard then cleared his throat as he looked toward Jack and then at Katrina. "Yes, Mommy is in heaven. She is looking down at us now and wants you to be a good girl."

"Oh, I will, Daddy." She looked up at the ceiling and in a delightful voice said, "Mommy, I will be good for you. Keep watching me! I love you!" Lizzy blew a kiss heaven-bound.

Katrina was taken back and noticed Mr. Whitaker had tears in his eyes. As she looked over at Jack, she noticed he had a look of gentleness. At the same time, Jack looked her way and looked directly into her eyes. Katrina felt awkward and looked away. She felt a flush in her cheeks. And at the same time, she felt a gentle breeze. She wondered where the air current was coming from and glanced around the room. She noticed a curtain blowing gently from one of the windows and figured the breeze must have come from there.

Just then there was a thud and footsteps as Johnny came bounding into the dining room. "Dad, Jack, come quick! There're a couple of men out front. They asked for Daddy. I don't likes the looks of them."

Mr. Whitaker turned to Johnny. "You mean you don't like the looks of them."

"That's what I said," replied Johnny with a frustrating smirk on his face.

"Yes, you did. I was correcting your grammar. You said 'I don't likes the looks.' The word 'like' never has an *s* at the end."

"Daddy, this is not the time to correct my grammar. I am serious about these guys. Hurry, come on."

Jack looked at Mr. Whitaker then at Johnny and was the first to respond. "Come on, Johnny." Jack put his hand on Johnny's shoulder and turned him back toward the door, "Let's go check out what they want. But stay on the porch," stated Jack as they left the room. Mr. Whitaker got up from his knees and headed toward the door.

Lizzy ran over to Katrina. "Is everything going to be all right?"

Katrina leaned over to Lizzy and put her arms around her. "Everything will be fine. Don't you worry. Why don't you go to the kitchen and see if you can get a cookie? If Olivia asks why, tell her because I said you're a good girl. Go on now," encouraged Katrina as she placed a hand on Lizzy's shoulders and gave her a gentle nudge out of the room. Katrina followed her out of the room. Lizzy went toward the kitchen as Katrina went toward the front door.

Jack and Mr. Whitaker were standing on the stone pathway near the hitching post. There were two men who had dismounted their horses, and they were standing on the dirt roadway on the other side of the white gated fence. Katrina heard some voices that sounded agitated. Katrina tried to get Johnny's attention to get him on the porch just in case he needed to be out of the way. Johnny was not looking toward her. He was standing next to his daddy. Jack had heard Katrina walk out on the porch and looked her way. He noticed that she was pointing toward Johnny then pointing to the porch. He understood what she was trying to get at. He leaned toward Johnny but not enough, as Mr. Whitaker could still hear. "Johnny, please go up on the porch and protect Katrina."

Johnny looked toward Katrina then back at Jack, and then he glanced over at his daddy. Mr. Whitaker nodded his head, and Johnny stepped back then went up on the porch and stood next to Katrina.

At that time, Jack pivoted toward the men, and Mr. Whitaker moved to stand in the view of Johnny and the men. Katrina draped her arm around Johnny as he came beside her on the porch. She wasn't sure what to expect with the confrontation by the gate.

Jack went through the gate to be on the side of the fence with the men who rode in. Mr. Whitaker stayed on the side of the fence near the house. The one man with the red flannel shirt started to walk up to Jack. Jack reached for his side arm. Mr. Whitaker raised his right hand and said to Jack, "Hold on, I don't want that kind of trouble." Jack dropped his arm to his side.

Mr. Whitaker turned to the other person standing near one of the horses that these two strangers rode in on. "Just what is it that ya'll want?"

The man in the red flannel shirt moved over near his partner. "We are looking for Mr. Martin and heard we might find him here."

"What is it that you want with Mr. Martin?" inquired Jack.

"It is our understanding that Mr. Martin is selling his farm, and we're interested. So if you can tell us where he is, we would like to talk to him." The redheaded man who spoke started to enter the gate.

Jack stepped in front of the gate to stop him. "Mr. Martin is not here, and he has changed his mind about selling his farm so you might as well just get on your horses and leave."

The man with the beard looked over to Mr. Whitaker and asked, "What do you have to say?"

Jack wondered if the man thought Mr. Whitaker was Mr. Martin. He decided not to tell them any different.

Mr. Whitaker responded, "What the young man said is true."

Both men hesitated then got on their horses and rode away.

Jack looked at Mr. Whitaker and stated, "For some reason, I don't think that will be the last that we will see of them. They gave me the creeps. Johnny, I want you to stay near the house. Don't go off gallivanting. Those men may be hanging around."

They all returned to the house. As they entered the main room, Amelia walked in from the hallway. "Supper is ready," stated Amelia as she turned and entered the dining room. Mr. Whitaker looked at the boys and said, "Time to wash up." They headed down the hall past the dining room.

Katrina went up the stairs to her room to wash up. As she came out of her room, she saw Lizzy standing at the top of the stairs. Lizzy looked up at Katrina and said, "I'm hungry. Aren't you?" She gave a slight smile. "Crying makes me hungry"—she hesitated—"and tired." She took Katrina's hand as Katrina started down the stairs. They walked together into the dining room.

Jack looked up as they entered the room and noticed Katrina and Lizzy holding hands. He started to grin as he was thinking about how Katrina seemed to be fitting in. Jack started to feel like he had butterflies in his stomach. He realized he was still looking at Katrina and glanced over to his father. Mr. Whitaker was also smiling as he was watching Jack's expression. Mr. Whitaker knew what was going on.

As Katrina and Lizzy entered the dining room, Lizzy blurted out, "They got washed before us." Then she climbed into her chair and placed her little hand on her daddy's hand. "Poppa, can Katrina stay with us? I like her."

With a smile on Mr. Whitaker's face, he leaned toward Lizzy and said, "Have you asked Katrina?"

Without hesitation, Katrina started to say, "I would . . ."

Lizzy turned to Katrina. "Will you please stay?"

Katrina looked over at Mr. Whitaker then at Jack. Lizzy noticed that Katrina looked at her Poppa and Jack and quickly spoke up, "Oh, don't worry about them. They want you to stay too."

With a look of surprise, Jack stated, "How do you know that?"

Lizzy chuckled and then with a giggle said, "Easy. You like her. And Poppa said I need to have a wo-woman around to look after me 'cause he said he doesn't know how to handle me."

Mr. Whitaker, with a smirk on his face said, "Well aren't we a presumptuous little one." Lizzy looked at her Poppa with a quizzical glint, "What does pres . . . sump . . . tuous mean?"

Everyone started to laugh. Lizzy also laughed. Just then Amelia came in with a tray of soup. To change the conversation, Katrina said the soup smelled divine, and everyone chimed in, "Yes, it does."

As everyone started to eat their soup, Lizzy turned to Katrina and once again asked her, "Are you going to stay?"

Katrina, after finishing her spoonful of soup, responded, "For a while," and took another spoonful.

Chapter 10

The sun was flickering in the window of Katrina's bedroom as she was waking. She stretched and climbed out of the high bed, sliding to the floor. As her feet touched the rug, she remembered she was at the Whitaker house. Then she glanced over at the dress she had laid out the night before and remembered that it was the day of Mrs. Whitaker's funeral. Thoughts were swimming around in her mind. *Why am I here? What a difference from being in Pennsylvania to Uncle Tom's to being here at the Whitaker ranch. Is this my destination? What a journey in such a brief period of time. And the people who have entered my life: Jack, Uncle Tom, Lizzy, Mr. Whitaker, and Johnny.*

Just at that moment, there was a knock at her door. She answered, "Hello."

Lizzy was on the other side. "Are you up?"

"Yes."

Lizzy started to open the door just as Katrina heard Jack say, "Lizzy, don't disturb Katrina." Lizzy closed the door, and Katrina heard her comment to Jack, "I need Katrina to help me get dressed."

Katrina reminded herself that with no mother or Mrs. Beechwood, it seemed Lizzy was helpless. She then realized she had her work cut out for herself. "I'll be out in about ten minutes. Then I'll help you, Lizzy. Okay?"

Lizzy almost shouted, "I'll be in my room waiting," as she walked away from the door.

Katrina heard a door close and then heard footsteps descending the stairs. *Now to get myself dressed,* she thought.

As Katrina and Lizzy descended the stairs, they noticed a crowd in the entryway and folks going in and out of the parlor. Just as they reached the bottom step, Mr. Whitaker entered the room from the hall. As he glanced around the room, he stopped when he saw his Lizzy. It dawned on him that she looked so much like her mother. And she looked like a little girl so scared of what was happening. Then he saw Katrina; she was holding Lizzy's hand. He thanked the Lord for bringing Katrina into their lives. He wasn't sure how he would be handling Lizzy without her.

Mr. Whitaker walked over to his daughter and took her hand. At the same time, Johnny came up from behind and took Lizzy's other hand. Together they strolled into the parlor and walked over to the casket. The mahogany lid was up. There was a two-step bench in front of the casket. Lizzy started to step up as her father and brother helped her on the bench so she could be tall enough to see over the side of the coffin. Lizzy saw her mother's face, and a tear streaked down her cheek. She reached for her mother's hand and laid her little fingers on top.

Katrina stood in the doorway watching this scene and felt a heart-wrenching grip in her chest. She reached her hand over her chest and let out a gasp.

Jack was by the coffin, and he noticed Katrina's movements. He wanted to reach out to her. Just at that time, Mr. Whitaker started crying and had let go of his daughter's hand. Jack noticed this too and reached over to his father. It had been a long time since he touched his father. And to reach out to him now . . . He realized how much he missed this family life.

While this was taking place, Katrina noticed that Lizzy had turned to her father as had Johnny. She started toward them and saw when Jack reached toward Mr. Whitaker. She also saw that Mr. Whitaker put his hand on top of Jack's hand then walked away. That's when she noticed the hurt, the sadness in Jack's eyes.

Lizzy stepped down, and Johnny helped her. They were both wiping tears from their eyes. Katrina went to them and put her hands on their shoulders as they were side by side of each other.

At that time, Jack came over to the three of them. He looked at Katrina and whispered to her as he leaned toward her, "I've got the little ones. Thanks." Jack steered the children over to wooden chairs that were lined along the wall and sat down with them. Amelia walked in and handed handkerchiefs to Jack and the children then turned and left the room.

Katrina was standing near the coffin. She wasn't sure what to do. She fidgeted with her skirt as she looked around the room. As she turned around, she suddenly realized that she was facing the coffin. As she looked down to see Mrs. Whitaker, she saw how beautiful she was. She knew then that Lizzy looked like her mother. Katrina thought, *She appeared to have been a fine lady. She must have fallen in love with Mr. Whitaker when she was young.*

Katrina started to wonder if she was Jack's mother but remembered Lizzy said his mother passed away. She wondered as she stood there, *What did his mother look like?* It dawned on her that she had been standing there for quite a while. She glanced around and saw more people coming into the room. She walked over towards Jack and the children when she noticed a beautiful, fancy-dressed young lady walk over to Jack and sit next to him. That left no place for Katrina to sit next to the children. She noticed a chair by the doorway and walked over to take a seat. At the same time, the clergyman walked toward the coffin and cleared his throat.

Jack noticed Katrina take a seat next to the door. *That's not where she's supposed to be*, he thought. Lizzy stood up at that time and looked around the room. As she saw Katrina, she shouted out, "Katrina, you're supposed to be here with us."

Katrina motioned to Lizzy to take a seat and calmly whispered across the room, "It's okay, honey."

Jack stood up at that moment and motioned with his hand for Katrina to take his seat. He stepped over toward his father and stood behind him. At the same time, Johnny moved to Jack's seat so Katrina could sit next to Lizzy.

As Katrina moved to her new seat, she noticed the young lady's look of discontent, and she turned her body away from Johnny. Johnny noticed and put a smile on his face as he leaned toward Lizzy and put his arm around his sister then moved back to make room for Katrina in between them.

Lizzy took Katrina's right hand and held it. She gave Katrina's hand a squeeze then leaned her body next to her friend.

Jack noticed all that as it took place and gave a slight smile as he glanced over to his father. He noticed that his father had witnessed this also and that he also smiled just as the clergyman started the service.

When all was over, Katrina stayed seated with the children. People were walking by as they went to Jack and Mr. Whitaker to give their condolences. No one addressed the children. Katrina decided to take them out of the room. She knew there were cookies in the dining room along with punch and was sure Johnny and Lizzy were parched.

As they stood to leave the room, Jack started to walk over but was intercepted. The young, beautiful lady that Katrina saw earlier met Jack in the middle of the room between them. She walked right up to Jack and put her arms around his left arm and sashayed herself and Jack right out the door of the room.

As they were leaving the room, Jack looked over his shoulder toward Katrina and the children with a startling look and raised his eyebrows. Mr. Whitaker happened to notice this and proceeded to walk over to Jack. As he reached the couple, he took the lady's hand and raised it as he lowered his head to kiss the back side of the hand.

"Constance, it's so nice to see you. Thank you for coming," spoke Mr. Whitaker as he continued to hold her hand, which made her drop Jack's arm. Mr. Whitaker picked up her arm at the elbow and started out the room with Constance by his side as he spoke to Jack, "Please check on the children for me, Jack, as I talk with the folks. Thank you."

Jack took the opportunity that his father had presented for him to not be with Constance. He turned around and walked back to the children and Katrina across the room with a smile on his face. Jack knew what his father was doing. He approached Lizzy and picked her up and carried her to the dining room with Katrina and Johnny following him.

After having some refreshments, Katrina noticed that Lizzy was yawning, and she suggested that Lizzy take a nap. Katrina looked at

Jack to let him know she was taking Lizzy upstairs to rest. Johnny overheard and announced that he was not tired but wanted to go outside.

Jack acknowledged Katrina's statement and then turned to Johnny. "I'm with you, Johnny. Come on." They all left the dining room with the boys heading toward the kitchen to leave the house and the girls going toward the backstairs that were used by the servants. Lizzy asked Katrina why they were going that way, and Katrina responded, "So no one sees us going upstairs, honey." They ascended the stairs.

Once in Lizzy's room, she yawned again as she stretched her arms wide and then up in the air above her head. She then crawled up on the davenport in the corner of the bedroom. Next to the seat was a large bookcase full of all sizes of books. Lizzy glanced over to the bookcase then at Katrina. "Will you read to me?" asked Lizzy.

"Of course, I would love to. What book would you like to hear?"

Lizzy shrugged her shoulder and replied, "You pick one. I love them all."

Katrina reached for a book on the second shelf and sat on the stool next to the davenport. As she positioned herself and leaned toward Lizzy, she opened the book to read. Lizzy settled her head down on the pillow so she could see the pages. Just as Katrina turned to the first page to read, Lizzy looked at Katrina and stated, "I love you, Katrina. Thank you for being here with me."

As she turned to look at Lizzy's innocent face, Katrina started to feel a tear swell up and a feeling of pride in her chest. She responded to Lizzy, "You are very welcome. Thank you for allowing me to be here with you and your family." Katrina turned back to the book and started to read the first page of *Jack and the Beanstalk*. As she went to turn to the next page, Katrina glanced over and saw that Lizzy was already fast asleep with a smile on her face. Katrina put the book down on the top of the bookcase as gingerly as she could and tiptoed out of the room.

Katrina decided to go to her room to freshen up and then she went down the front stairs and noticed the parlor was still full of neighbors. As she turned toward the parlor, she saw that Mr.

Whitaker's study had quite a few men sitting around smoking while chatting back and forth with each other. Katrina walked down the hall to the dining room and saw that there were women and children milling around the table filled with food.

Katrina decided to go outside to get away from it all. She strolled out the backdoor and walked past the outbuildings. She walked along the pasture's wooden fence and felt the sun on her face along with a warming wisp of air blowing her hair. Then a brief gust of wind made its presence known, and Katrina thought about her father and how he would have loved to be here with her and how proud he would be of how she had managed all the trials and tribulations she had endured so far in her life. She thought about how it was a rough road, but she felt now that she was ready to settle down in her new life.

As Katrina was inhaling the fresh air and marveling at God's beautiful sights, she felt another brief gust of wind and turned to see where it was coming from. There stood Jack looking directly at her. Without realizing it, she blushed. Jack noticed the rosy cheeks and smiled. His smile made Katrina feel warm inside.

Jack approached her and held his hand out to her as he said, "I have something to show you." She took his hand without hesitation and walked with him. They walked silently together to a path that went alongside the meadow and then next to a small set of woods. As the path narrowed, so did the field. Another set of woods descended upon them as the field disappeared. Jack remarked, "We're almost there. I want to show you something that is truly beautiful. A piece of work that the Lord gave us here on this ranch."

As Jack spoke, the woods began to give way to a clearing. In the clearing was a luscious green field filled with flowers that were in every color under the rainbow. This field was surrounded by rocky hills, and among the rocks, Katrina saw the most precious, small waterfalls that she had ever seen. There were several waterfalls varying in height, and these tiny falls were beautiful, with miniature pools of water at the foot of each one.

Katrina drew in a breath then commented, "This is spectacular." Her blue-green eyes were wide open and you could see the reflection of this view in her eyes.

"Do others know about this place?" she asked as she turned to Jack.

Jack walked closer to her, "So what do you think? This is a very special place."

Katrina had gone back to looking at the view as she didn't want to take her eyes off from it. "It is so beautiful. Who owns this piece of paradise?" she inquired.

Jack responded, "I do." He continued talking as he looked around with a dreamy look on his face. "I've always dreamt about building a cabin along there," as he pointed toward the woods that stood behind them, to the edge of the field where it backed up to the woods close to where they came through the path. "I figured here I would have the best view of the falls. It would be such a wonderful panoramic view."

"Yes, it would be," agreed Katrina. "What a perfect place."

Jack noticed Katrina's smile on her face and felt the warmth of her standing next to him. Jack felt very pleased and happy. He liked this feeling.

Katrina took a deep breath and felt a peace about her. Then suddenly, she felt another gust of wind. She knew her father was there and he would have approved of this place. Without thinking, she spoke to her father out loud. "Father, this is why you came here, isn't it? I just remembered that you said something about a place of paradise in one of your letters."

Jack heard her and put his arms around her shoulder as he turned her toward him.

"Yes, Katrina your father knew of this place. He's the one who showed it to me."

Katrina looked up and into Jack's eyes. She saw a love and glean in his brown eyes that made her feel very comfortable and content.

Jack continued talking while keeping his arms around her. He looked squarely into her face again as he said, "Your father wanted to keep this separated from the farm. He didn't want to disturb the beauty of this land."

"I can understand how he felt. Being here right now, I feel the same way." She hesitated then looked at Jack, "Do you feel that way too, Jack?"

"Yes, I do feel this is a special place." replied Jack. "And *Katrina*, this was your father's place, his land. You should know he sold it to me." Before he could say anything more, Katrina promptly responded to his statement.

"What?" Katrina couldn't believe her ears. "Why did he sell it?" asked Katrina.

Jack saw the disappointment in Katrina's face as she turned away from him.

"Katrina, he didn't want it taken away if he ended up losing the farm and we agreed for me to have it to be safe."

Katrina knew what Jack said made sense but she felt a tinge of jealousy. She thought about how this would have been her land if father hadn't sold it to Jack.

As Katrina stood watching the awesome view of the falls, Jack turned her again towards him and put his arms around her. She turned toward him without hesitation and when she was facing him, she felt another gust of wind, a soft gentle breeze that felt like a hand touching her cheek.

Jack looked straight into Katrina's eyes and she looked back into his. She felt like it was a long time that they stood looking at each other when it really was a matter of seconds. Katrina noticed once again the brown, starry eyes of the man who has been on her mind many times since her train ride into Widow's Peak. She started to feel woozy and light-headed then she suddenly felt Jack's strong hands on her back, supporting her, helping her to stay on her feet, to stay strong. She realized he was the pillar of her strength since she had been here and it felt good. She decided this was not the time to question her situation about the land. She felt secure and knew that Jack truly cared about her. Without realizing it she placed her right hand on his shoulder and looked again into his eyes.

Jack took his hands and arms from her back and grasped both of her shoulders with both of his hands and pulled her toward him. He felt he couldn't stop himself now. He knew he wanted to place his lips on hers. He saw that her eyes were gleaming and soft looking. He continued to lean his face to her face and then their lips met. Jack felt her soft lips and gently kissed them. As he continued to kiss her, he realized she was kissing him back. His heart soared. He felt like he was in heaven. *Lord this is wonderful. Katrina is wonderful*, he thought.

Katrina's mind was racing with thoughts about how soft his lips were and how gentle he was in holding her. She felt like she was going to melt, yet she didn't pull away. She decided she liked how she was feeling and she didn't want it to end. Suddenly, she realized he was standing there and he wasn't kissing her, he was watching her. She didn't realize she had her eyes closed. As she looked again into his eyes, he started to say, "I'm sor—" Before he could finish, Katrina put her right-hand index finger to his mouth. She didn't want anything to disturb the moment.

"Jack, I love this place, I can understand why you bought it to keep it safe." As she stated this she turned toward the falls, "This place is mesmerizing and breathtaking." She turned back around toward him, "and so are you." She looked again into his eyes.

Jack replied, "I would love to stay here with you, but we'd better get back to the house. Father, I mean, Mr. Whitaker, may need me."

Katrina decided she had to know, "Is he your father?"

Jack looked at her, "Yes, but it's a long story."

They started walking back toward the house in silence.

Chapter 11

A s Jack returned to the house after being out in the field most of the day, he approached the barn and noticed some horses by the corral that he hadn't seen before. He walked toward the house and noticed Katrina walking back from the outhouse. He walked up to her and escorted her to the back door. As Katrina entered through the doorway, she heard the door close and turned to see Jack heading toward the barn.

As she surveyed the scene, she noticed a man on the side of the barn peering around the corner as Jack reached the main doors. She saw the man draw a gun slowly from his side. She started to panic then realized she had to warn Jack. She opened the door just as she saw another man in a long coat come around from the other side of the barn with a rifle. It dawned on her that these were the men that came to the house a while ago and was looking for her uncle. She noticed the red flannel shirt and the man with the long coat.

Before she opened the door fully, she ran to the parlor hoping that Mr. Whitaker was there. She saw him sitting in a parlor chair talking to a man. She went over and whispered into his ear, "There are two men by the barn with guns and Jack is out there." That's all she said. Mr. Whitaker jumped out of his chair and said to the man sitting next to him, "Come on Mike." They went out the front door as Katrina went back into the kitchen to look out the back door.

She saw the one man take his gun and hit Jack on the back of his head. The second man started to raise his gun toward Jack then Katrina saw the man turn toward the house. Then he started to run around the side of the barn and she heard a shot; then saw the man that was running stop and put his hands in the air as he dropped his gun. The man who hit Jack in the head started to stumble to his knees at the same time she heard the shot. While this all took place, Jack slumped to the ground in front of the barn door.

Katina prayed aloud, "Oh no! Please God let him be all right. Please help Jack!"

Katrina saw the man Mr. Whitaker called Mike run up to the one man and seized the long gun and at the same time Mr. Whitaker retrieved the pistol from the ground next to the fellow kneeling on the ground.

Katrina ran out the door and over to Jack as quickly as she could. She noticed the blood in Jack's hair. She turned Jack's face from the dirt and cupped his face in both of her hands. Just then Jack's eyes fluttered and he let out a groan.

She heard Mr. Whitaker, "Good job sheriff. These are two of the three men I saw in town. They were boasting about getting Mr. Tom Martin's property."

The sheriff asked, "Where is Tom?"

That's when Mr. Whitaker noticed Katrina kneeling and holding the head of someone lying on the ground. He then realized it was Jack and he ran over to them and knelt beside Katrina. As he leaned over, he noticed Jack's face was bloody near the top and he felt the area of Jack's head where the blood was coming from. There was a large bump. Then Mr. Whitaker checked for a pulse on Jack's throat and whispered, "He's alive. Let's get him in the house then someone needs to get the doctor for us."

During this time, Katrina sat next to Jack and watched Mr. Whitaker. A couple of hired hands came running over. One of them said, "We heard a shot!" They saw Jack on the ground. "Come on men, let's get him in the house. Mr. Whitaker and Katrina stepped aside to let the hired hands pick Jack up. Katrina wanted to help but knew she would only be in the way. They carried Jack into the dining room.

In the meantime, the sheriff corralled the men who attacked Jack with the help of another couple of hired hands. The sheriff climbed on the wagon along with a hired hand from the ranch. They headed to town with the criminals tied in the wagon and their horses tied to the back of the wagon. Three more of the hired hands went with the sheriff to help ensure they reached the jail.

In the meantime, Katrina entered the house through the kitchen door. As she closed the door, Johnny came from the window and reached for Katrina's arm. "What's happening?" he cried.

Katrina told Johnny what she knew. She noticed his worried face and put her arms around Johnny, "Don't worry Johnny, he'll be all right. He's strong." As they walked toward the parlor, Uncle Tom walked in the front door.

Katrina looked at Uncle Tom and stated to him, "Uncle Tom, Jack's been hurt."

"I heard," responded Uncle Tom. "I was in the barn and heard the commotion. Where's Jack?" he questioned as he started toward the parlor.

"He's in here," remarked Mr. Whitaker as he came out from the dining room. "I'm going to get some water and a cloth to clean up the blood." Mr. Whitaker headed toward the kitchen just as Amelia came from her room right off from the hall near the kitchen. Mr. Whitaker walked into the kitchen with Amelia and as they entered the room he was asking her to get some cloth for bandages. Johnny followed his father, "I'll help you too father."

Katrina followed her uncle into the dining room. Jack had been placed on the table. Katrina noticed a man standing over Jack then heard Uncle Tom talking to the man wearing a grey suit. "How is he Doc?"

The man turned to glance at Katrina. She noticed that he looked old in the face with lots of deep wrinkles. She surmised that he would be wise and know what he is doing if he has been doctoring for most of his life. She prayed for the Lord to give this old man the skill and steady hands to help Jack.

As Doc resumed checking Jack's chest and head, he replied, "He will be fine. He's as strong as an ox. The bump on his head has started to go down." The elderly gentlemen moved his hand to Jack's bump and as he touched it, Katrina noticed the squinted face that Jack made. She wondered how Jack could endure the pain that he must be feeling after the beating he received. Doc made another comment, "And the bleeding has stopped."

"I am so glad you were close by here Doc Beavers. Thank you," remarked Tom as he turned from the table and looked at Katrina. "Jack will be in good hands."

Doc Beavers turned and reached for his coat on the oak chair nearest to him and stepped away as he put his brown corduroy coat on. "There's not much to do for him right now other than to get him in bed and keep him down for a few days. The swelling needs to be completely gone before he's up and at 'em." The doctor turned to look at Mr. Whitaker and Johnny, who had just entered the room, as he stated, "That's Doc's orders!"

Just then Jack let out a moan and reached his right hand to his head. He flinched as he touched the lump on the top of his head. His eyes were still closed. Jack started to whisper something. The doctor leaned over Jack's face with his ear to Jack's lips to hear. Again, Jack said something. The doctor heard him say "Katrina." The doctor turned his head toward Katrina as he raised his head, "Katrina?"

"Yes," she replied and started walking toward the table.

"It will be your job to watch Jack and change the cloth on his wound periodically. Be sure it stays clean. And don't let this man go anywhere after he's moved to his bedroom."

"Okay," responded a hesitant nurse to be. Katrina hoped that she would be able to handle Jack. Katrina nodded her head as a sign of understanding. Mr. Whitaker turned to Johnny and asked him to fetch a couple of the hands to come into the house to help Jack to his bed upstairs.

Katrina's head started to drop down as she was sitting in the rather large easy chair in Jack's room. She had been watching him most of the night. When she opened her eyes, she remembered she was still in Jack's room. She threw off the blanket on her lap and draped it over the arm of the chair. As she stood and stretched, she peered over towards Jack lying in his bed. She noticed he had beads of sweat on his forehead. She wondered if he still had a fever or was it gone now. She went over to the side of the bed and reached out to touch Jack's forehead. She determined that he was a little warm and believed he may have already sweated most of the fever out of his body. She reached over to the stand holding a bowl of water and took the cloth from the bowl and wrung it out then turned back toward Jack. She put the cloth on his forehead to absorb the beads of sweat and turned back toward the water bowl to rewet the cloth. As she turned around to wipe his face and the cloth touched his cheek, he smiled, then he moaned and squinted his face from pain. Jack opened his eyes and looked at Katrina; this time with another smile as he tried to lift his head from the pillow.

"Jack, don't move. Please keep your head down. You have quite a large bump and bruise on your head. You will recover sooner if you stay down for a while."

Jack smiled again and then closed his eyes as he asked her what time it was. She replied, "Early morning."

Jack asked another question as he turned his head to one side. "How long have I been sleeping?"

"Two days," Katrina responded.

"Who else has been here?" inquired Jack.

"Your father and Uncle Tom have been in to see how you're doing. Johnny and Elizabeth have popped in to check on you. They are the only ones who have been here." At that time, Katrina put the cloth back in the bowl and took a towel to dry his face as she continued to talk. "There have been a lot of folks asking about you according to your father."

When she finished drying his face, he opened his eyes up again and looked directly at her. "How long have you been here?" he questioned. Then he closed his eyes tight and reopened them. "My head really hurts," he exclaimed.

"It will probably hurt for a few more days. Apparently, the man who hit you with the gun was very strong and forceful." Katrina didn't want to let him know that she had been with him the whole time. To avoid his question, she continued talking. "The sheriff arrested the men who had stopped here and were asking about Uncle Tom's land a while back. They were the same ones who were here trying to find out more about Uncle Tom's land when you surprised them out by the barn."

Jack responded with another look of pain as he stated, "Glad they got the men." There was silence for a moment. Then Jack looked back at Katrina for a second time and asked, "So how long have you been here?"

Katrina started to look away then felt a breeze, a brief gust of air, and looked over to see if the window was open. It wasn't open. Jack noticed Katrina look toward the window. He reached for her hand which was near his bedside just as she looked back at him when he touched her hand.

Jack looked at her face and asked, "Is it your father again?"

"What?" asked Katrina. This was another question she wanted to avoid answering. She felt like he could read her thoughts.

Jack squeezed her hand and asked once again, "How long?"

She decided to answer him so he would stop asking. "Since they brought you to your room. I wanted to make sure you were going to be okay. And, besides, the doctor asked me to take care of you . . . I mean your wound." Katrina looked away as she gave her answer.

Just at that time, Jack squeezed her hand again and said, "Thank you. When I am up and about, I owe you dinner."

"No, you don't, Jack. Just get better and take me back to the beautiful waterfalls." This time Katrina squeezed his hand and then she let go as the door opened with a creaking noise and at the same time there was a light knocking on the wood.

Mr. Whitaker walked in at the same time Katrina let go of Jack's hand and moved away from the bed. Jack moved his hand to his chest. Mr. Whitaker saw all of this and gave a quick, silent thank you to the Lord and proceeded to the side of Jack's bed as Katrina stepped away.

Mr. Whitaker looked at Katrina and said to her, "You don't have to go."

Katrina responded, "Yes, I do. I need a break and will get some fresh water for Jack." She left the room before Mr. Whitaker could reply. Mr. Whitaker turned to face Jack as the door closed and said, "You have the best nurse, you know."

Jack smiled as he looked toward the door and remarked, "I know!" Then Jack looked at his father. "What about the men that were caught? Katrina told me the sheriff got them."

"Yes, he did and one finally told Sheriff Wheeler that another one was hiding on Tom's property. They're still looking for him.

In a panic, Jack asked, "What about Tom?"

"He's fine," replied his father. "He was here in the barn when you were hit on the head. He knows what happened and has been helping in the search." Just then they heard a commotion from downstairs and then footsteps running up the stairs. The bedroom door flew open as Johnny pounced into the room. "Father, Mr. Martin's been wounded. Where's Katrina?"

"What?" responded Jack with an alarmed sound to his voice. Jack tried to sit up. Mr. Whitaker placed his hand over Jack's chest and slightly pushed Jack back down on the bed.

"Johnny, stay here with Jack." Mr. Whitaker looked at Jack and stated, "I'll find out what is going on." Mr. Whitaker left the room quickly.

Johnny turned to look at Jack, "Well, you're finally awake!"

Katrina entered the kitchen and went to pour water into a glass from the pitcher sitting on the table. As she turned and went into the hallway, she started to pass the dining room and heard voices. She paused by the door which was slightly open. She cocked her head so her ear was closer to the door opening to be able to hear the conversation. She heard Uncle Tom make a statement, "We have to do something with those men. If they're let go, they'll just come back and cause more trouble."

Then Katrina heard the sheriff speak. "I sent a message off to Fort Hanover. I'm waiting to find out if those men are wanted elsewhere and if so, what for."

Then Mr. Whitaker spoke. "I hope they are. That will make it easier to put them away, and hopefully for good."

She heard Uncle Tom again, "Thank God they didn't kill Jack."

Mr. Whitaker spoke immediately stating, "And thank God they didn't kill you. How's your arm doing?"

"I'm okay. Someone went to get the doc. He should be here soon."

Katrina heard this and opened the door. They looked at her. "Tom will be fine. The bullet scraped his arm."

"Bullet?" questioned Katrina.

"Yah, the bullet nicked me but we got the last man." replied Uncle Tom. "Don't worry about me, I'll be just fine."

Katrina felt weak in the knees. She didn't want to fall and figured she had heard enough. She knew if Uncle Tom said he was fine, he meant it. She went to the stairs to climb them and realized just how tired she really was. As she climbed the stairway she decided she should turn in for the night. She knocked on Jack's door and heard him say to come in. She went over to the side of his bed and set the glass of water down on the night stand. She checked Jack's wound. Jack just watched her. She tried to not make eye contact and after checking his head, she said, "Good, no bleeding. Just get some rest now." She turned and left the room. Jack laid there quietly. Katrina turned back to look at Jack when she reached the door. "Jack, I am so glad that you are okay. I'm exhausted and will turn in now myself. Good night." She didn't wait for a reply. She stepped out and closed the door.

She was anxious to lay down in the comfort of her bed. Once she was in her room she remembered that she should change the water in the basin in Jack's room first. As she opened the door to Jack's room, she noticed the lamp was lit so she knocked before fully opening the door. She heard a voice that wasn't Jack's. It dawned on her that it was Johnny in the room. He stood up and glanced her way as she stepped in the room. He put his index finger to his mouth and said, "Shh, Jack's almost asleep. You go on to bed. I'll stay with him tonight." Katrina thanked Johnny and proceeded to her room.

Chapter 12

As she laid in bed she thought about all the things that have happened to her since she arrived in Widow's Peak. While thinking back, it dawned on her that she never got a reply to the message she had sent shortly after she arrived. She wondered if it was pertinent now. Should she still inquire about the money owed to her from the New York endeavor or leave well enough alone. But it still bugged her, wondering why she didn't hear anything from her request. It seemed like years ago when it was only a few months. She wondered if that was really a wise thing to do, sending the message and now following up with it. She realized she had to decide and move on or she wouldn't be able to go forward in her life. She really dreaded bringing her past to the present. However, she knew that if she didn't resolve things from the past, then she had no future here or with Jack. *What!?!?! With Jack? Was that possible? Did she really feel that way about Jack?* Katrina's mind raced with questions of concern.

Oh, dear Lord, help me to make the right decision, to be able to move on and feel good about my choices. I need your guidance. Please help me. And please help Jack to heal quickly. Help the sheriff, Uncle Tom and Mr. Whitaker to convict the corrupt men so they are put away for good and not hurt anyone else. I know you want us to forgive but how can I forgive those men? Especially after they hurt Jack; they almost killed him. And my uncle. Is that what you expect from your people? I'm a confused person and hope that you can guide me in the right direction. Thank you, Lord, in the name of your son Jesus Christ. Katrina pulled the covers up to her shoulders as she turned to her side to fall asleep.

As Katrina entered the dining room for breakfast, she noticed Uncle Tom sitting in a chair with a bandage wrapped around his arm helping to hold his arm up toward his shoulder and his hand over his chest. She quickly went to him and bent down near him. "What happened, Uncle Tom?" She was concerned about her uncle and wanted to help him. After all, he was her only family there.

"I had a bullet graze my arm. Remember hearing about it last night?"

Katrina remembered as he spoke. At that time, Mr. Whitaker walked into the dining room and sat in his chair at the end of the table. As he reached for his napkin and placed it on his lap, he looked up to Tom. "I hope you're feeling some better today, Tom."

"I could be better. The arm is paining me some right now." replied Tom.

As Katrina wrung her hands together she asked, "Please tell me what really happened. How did you get shot?" She pulled up a chair next to Uncle Tom.

At that very moment, Jack entered the room with his hand holding the bandage on his head. He took the seat next to Katrina and sat down. He looked at Tom. "What happened to you, Tom?" inquired Jack.

"Well, we found the third man who was hiding last night, or should I say he found me!" answered Tom to Jack. He continued, "I was with Mike Wheeler last night as we were searching my land when this big fella jumped from behind a tree. He tried to attack me then took off. As he was running away, he turned and fired his handgun at me."

Katrina gasped as she watched Uncle Tom telling this story. She was about to stand up when her uncle motioned for her to stay seated and continued talking.

"The sheriff was off to the side, near this man, and he grabbed him while his deputy came from behind them and was able to help take the man down. Deputy Jim grabbed his wrist and put both hands behind his back as he was being handcuffed. I landed on the ground with the force that almost knocked the wind out of me. It all happened so quickly. He is now behind bars this morning. And, by the way, I am fine," replied Tom as he reached for the platter of eggs that were brought in as he was explaining the night's adventure. At that time, everyone dug in to eat breakfast. Not another word was spoken during breakfast.

Katrina knew that this wasn't the end of it and she was right as she heard later that morning when Uncle Tom and Mr. Whitaker talked about going to a court hearing.

Katrina felt out of sorts with all that had taken place in just a few short days. She felt confined and stressed. She decided to take a ride into town. She figured maybe that would help her to unwind some and give her a chance to sort out her thoughts.

As Katrina knocked on the open door to the den, she felt an urgency to scream. She knew she really needed to get away. She entered the den hoping that her knocking was heard as she didn't want to startle anyone. She wondered if others were as wired as she felt.

Mr. Whitaker turned toward the door to acknowledge the knock and gave a big smile when he saw Katrina in the doorway. "Come in my dear. What can I do for you?"

Katrina entered the large room that held several leather chairs and a large oak desk. Two of the walls had full bookcases. *This is certainly a man's room,* she thought. She went to stand next to Mr. Whitaker as he was sitting at his large desk. "I was wondering if I could borrow the wagon or at least a horse."

"Of course, Katrina. Where do you plan to ride?" inquired Mr. Whitaker.

"I need to go into town."

Just at that time, Jack and Tom walked into the room and they heard her last statement. Before Jack could respond, Tom spoke up. "I would prefer you not go anywhere by yourself, Katrina." Mr. Whitaker nodded his head and said he agreed. Jack then offered to take Katrina.

Katrina knew that she couldn't change any of their minds but she wanted to be alone. She realized that wouldn't happen now. So, she responded with "Fine, I'll be ready in fifteen minutes then, okay?"

Jack looked at both Mr. Martin and his father, then back at Katrina. "Okay, meet you out front in fifteen," as he made his way out the door.

Katrina looked at both older men and said thank you then left the room to prepare to head into town.

The ride to town was uneventful. Both Katrina and Jack rode in silence. Each was in ones own thoughts. As they approached town it was like a clap of thunder woke them from their own hypnotic state. Jack noticed the Post Office at the same time Katrina did.

"Where do you need to go?" asked Jack to Katrina.

"The Post Office to start with," replied Katrina.

Jack pulled the wagon up to the Post Office boardwalk and jumped down from the wagon. Before Katrina could stand up, Jack was on her side of the wagon and reaching up to help her down. Jack looked in Katrina's eyes as he set her on the ground, releasing his hands from her waist.

"Katrina, I also have a couple of errands. I'll meet you back here in about an hour. Okay?"

"That's fine," replied Katrina.

Jack secured the horses and wagon and walked off toward the end of the street. Katrina entered the Post Office and went to a waist high table that held paper and pencils. She picked up a pencil and sheet of paper and began to write.

> *Dear Mr. Schenk, I'm writing to let you know that Mr. Martin, my uncle, and I are well. This note is to inform you that I will be remaining here at Widow's Peak. Therefore, would you please send me my valuables -- all of them. I do not plan to return to New York. All my attributes can be sent to my attention at my uncle's farm.*
>
> *Thank you for all your assistance.*
>
> *Katrina Martin.*

Katrina folded the paper and reached for an envelope when she thought about how she was going to explain things to her uncle when her belongings arrived. How would Jack feel? It will all workout. She was sure that they would understand.

She sealed the envelope and wrote the address on the front then went to the window to pay the Postmaster. She knew she still had time, so she walked out of the Post Office and went down the street and looked in windows of the few shops in Widow's Peak. The first shop was a dress shop. She noticed a flowery bonnet that had large white roses. *Not for me*, she thought. Her gaze went to the black lace shawl. It had a beautiful leaf pattern with lots of holes. *That surely won't keep me warm.* She continued looking in the window. Inside the shop, she saw a brown and green striped dress hanging on a mannequin. It was decorated with a beige collar that matched the cuffs of the bodice. Katrina thought it was a striking dress. While peering in the window, a few folks had walked by. Katrina didn't notice anyone since she was concentrating on the dress. It dawned on her that she was staring in the window. She turned to see who was looking. It was obvious, no one was paying attention to her. She moved on. She walked past a few shops then noticed the church at the end of the street. Katrina decided to go and check it out. It had been a long time since she had been to church. She realized it had been quite a while and she felt guilty.

"Sorry, Lord."

Katrina knew it took more than a sorry. She knew she needed to go to church. As she approached the building, she noticed the grass was tall and weedy. There were no flowers or bushes in the front. As she placed her right foot on the first step she heard a crack and saw the board start to break. "Oh, boy, these steps are not safe," she whispered. She gently proceeded up the steps and reached the front door. She then noticed that the glass in the door window was cracked. As she tried the doorknob, the door slowly opened with such a squeaking noise that it was irritating to her ears. As she peered inside, it was obvious no one had been inside for church services in quite a while. There was dust and cobwebs in many corners. Some of the pews were upside down and some were lying on their sides. The walls and ceiling were cracked and paint was peeling off the surfaces.

How awful, she thought. *Didn't anyone go to church?* She didn't see another church in town. "This is horrifying. Doesn't anyone believe in God in this town and worship him?" She questioned outloud even though there was no one within earshot to hear her.

There was a table next to the door that had a small pile of books. She went to see what the books were about. There was a pile of King James Bibles then she looked at the next set of books to find that they were readers and mathematics primers. This must have been the schoolhouse, too. Come to think of it, Katrina suddenly realized that she had not seen a school, nor had she heard of Mr. Whitaker's children going to school. She decided she had to ask Jack about all of this or maybe Uncle Tom. Katrina decided an hour must have passed and decided she better get back to the wagon.

Jack was at the wagon, waiting for her. He had been worried since she was nowhere in sight when he returned to the wagon, but he knew he'd better stay near the wagon. He then figured she was still busy and would be back and hated to not be by the wagon when she did return.

Jack helped Katrina climb up on the seat of the wagon, then positioned himself next to her as he reached for the reins to make the horses move.

Katrina decided to ask Jack about the church since she had to know about church services and school. It became a driving force within her, she had a strong yearning to know. Like a hope of connecting to her Lord. Katrina knew that this drive within her was very deep-rooted and she needed answers. She hoped that Jack could answer her questions.

"Jack?"

Jack was startled by Katrina's question; more so because he didn't expect her to say anything since they rode to town in silence.

"Yes?" replied Jack.

"What can you tell me about the church in town? Why is it abandoned? Is there another church? Is there a school?" questioned Katrina as she looked off into the land that was passing by.

"Whoa there. Why all the questions? Are you okay?" responded Jack.

Katrina looked at Jack and started to laugh then she was giggling.

Jack was really puzzled now. "What's so funny?" asked Jack.

"Me. I have had a revelation. But I need answers first. After looking in the church, I need to know what happened."

"Well, the town was prospering at one point. When gold was discovered out west, a lot of the folks left to find their riches. A few families stayed and did their best to keep things going, but it was a struggle. There weren't many children so no need for a school. Those with little ones taught them at home.

There was silence between the two of them. Katrina was looking off to the mountain. She noticed that it was a strange looking mountain. It was as tall as some of the buildings she had seen in Philadelphia. She wondered why "Widow's Peak." What happened here to have Widow's Peak as a name for a town.

"Jack, why the name Widow's Peak?" asked Katrina.

"When many of the men left to go find gold, they never returned. Many of the women went to the top of the mountain, watching for the men to come back to them." Jack pointed to the top of the small mountain. "The wives would take turns staying up there watching for their men to return. Most of the men never returned so most of the wives claimed themselves as widows. Folks would talk about the situation and next thing you know, everyone was referring to the area as "Widow's Peak."

"How sad," replied Katrina while still in the thought about the women folk climbing the mountain and watching from all angles waiting for a sign of their loved ones returning home.

Jack noticed how Katrina was staring off towards the peak of the mountain. He interrupted her thoughts, "I can't understand how a man could leave his wife and his family, let alone go and never return."

Katrina turned her head toward Jack. She looked at his face and saw that he looked so sincere. She then wondered why he didn't have a woman in his life. But, she didn't dare ask. That was not proper to inquire of such matters. Katrina thought, he must have had someone special in his life. She wondered what had happened. Maybe someday she will know.

Katrina's mind drifted back to the name of the town and thought that the name made the town seem more secluded and sad. Then she thought about the church.

"Jack, what happened to the church?" inquired Katrina.

Jack had stopped the wagon while they were in conversation. Katrina realized this. She turned to him. Jack turned to face Katrina. "My, you certainly are quizzical. Why all the questions? What is on your mind?" As he asked her these questions, he took her hands and placed his hands around hers. Katrina didn't pull back her hands. She felt the warmth of his hands while he was holding her hands. She became tingly all over then felt a gust of wind. As she felt the breeze, she knew her father was approving. She gave a shiver. Jack felt the shiver transfer from Katrina's hand through to his hands. He asked her if she was cold. Katrina responded, "No, I'm fine." At this same time, Jack had put his arm around her. He felt he couldn't help himself. He pulled her closer to him. He felt the warmth of her back and the heat that came between them. As he was pulling her closer he smelled the sweet scent of vanilla and then a wisp of her hair touched his face. He so wanted to hold her tight and to kiss her.

Katrina felt the warmth of Jack's arms around her and the sweet, rugged man-smell of Jack's body. She wanted to lean on him and put her head on his chest. She felt so safe in his arms, but fear ran through her mind. What am I doing. This is not proper, especially out here without a chaperone, so close to Jack, so much excitement running through her mind and body. While she was running all this through her head, she suddenly felt the warmth of his lips on her cheek, then on her lips. She wanted to pull away because her mind was saying to. But Katrina didn't back away. The light touch of Jack's lips on her sent a chill down her spine. A feeling that felt like sparks touching her and setting her on fire. She had a feeling that was extremely spectacular.

Jack was feeling a need to go further. He knew he had to stop now or regret his actions.

He didn't want to hurt her and didn't want to lose her. He thought, *Lord, help me to do this right. I need her in my life.*

He pulled away. "Katrina, I'm sorry." He saw her eyes were looking wild and excited. Then he saw her reach up to touch her lips, then she moved her hands to her hair, pretending to put a loose piece back away from her face. She then straightened herself up and faced the front of the wagon. Jack did the same thing. Neither spoke the rest of the way home but they both had a smile on their faces.

For the rest of the ride back to the ranch, Jack was deep in thought. He still wondered why all the questions from Katrina. Why the interest in the town's name? Why the interest in the people who have lived here, and especially the church that has been empty for the last twenty years or so? Then he started to think about her past. She said she came out here to help run the farm with her uncle. She was very upset to find out that he had an interest in the farm. Now she's helping at the Whitaker Ranch. Why did she really come here? Where did she come from? What was she doing before she came here?

Jack realized that he had never wondered about any of this before. But he did know he had feelings for her and they seem to get stronger each time he's with her. But, he couldn't help but wonder about her, this woman who he was having feelings for but was still a mystery to him. Jack decided he wanted to pursue this relationship. He knew he needed to take it one step at a time. He didn't want to push her away.

Katrina realized she still didn't know much about the church. She knew that she would have to wait for the right time to inquire further about Widow's Peak's church that sits empty and forlorn in the heart of town.

The ranch was coming into view as Katrina noticed that dusk was descending upon them. What a day, she thought, and just then, she felt another gust of wind. *Yes, father. Thank you for bringing me here.*

Please know that I would love to do something for my God. I feel I have been neglecting Him since I've come here and yet, I am starting to feel blessed.

Dear Lord, thank you for showing me the way. I need you as much now as I did when I was struggling in Pennsylvania. Please be by my side and guide me in what you want my future to be. Thank You, Amen.

Katrina realized that she felt refreshed and like a weight had been taken away from her. She knew from growing up, how important it is to have the Lord in her life. Why did she stray from it? She knew she needed God back in her life again. It dawned on her that she couldn't remember any of the Scriptures from the Bible that she learned as a child. She made a solemn vow to pick up the Bible and to start reading it again.

Chapter 13

Mr. Whitaker decided to take the children for a picnic. He wanted to spend the day with them. That morning he had asked Katrina if she wanted to join them. She knew that it would be better if he spent the time alone with Johnny and Lizzy. She had let Mr. Whitaker know that the children needed time just with him. She knew they were missing their mother.

Katrina was determined to go back to the farm. She wanted to check on the house and she wanted time to herself. She got a horse from the stable and she rode out. She had several things running through her mind. Before leaving she told Olivia that she was going for a ride and would be back by supper time.

As Katrina rode up to the house, she noticed a couple of horses by the barn. She quietly rode to the far side of the barn where she was out of sight. She dismounted and slid through the fence rail and tiptoed to the side of the barn where there was a window. She heard voices inside. Someone was moving about. Katrina knew that her uncle and Jack were out to the south pastures to check on some of the cattle that broke through the fence.

Knowing this, she wanted to know who was here and why. She moved closer to the barn window and heard a man talking. "Can't wait 'til Gus gets here. We can clean this place out so easy. Haven't seen any one come by here for a few days."

"I agree," replied another voice. "Gus says not to go near the house 'til he gits here, but I want to see what's in thar`."

"Better not, best to wait for Gus. You know how ornery he gets at times." said the first voice.

Katrina knew these men were up to no good. She wondered what she could do to stop this vandalism. Should she get Uncle Tom and Jack? Or should she ride into town for the sheriff? She didn't want to get Mr. Whitaker. Besides, she didn't know where he went with the children. She wondered how far Uncle Tom was, or would it be quicker to get the sheriff?

She knew she had to think quick. Katrina felt a gust of wind just as she thought about Jack. She then knew her father was telling her to find Jack. As she slowly walked back to the fence, the horses in front of the barn whinnied. The men in the barn had walked out the front door and looked at the horses then searched with their eyes over to the house and then over to the corral.

There was no wasting time now. If they saw Katrina, she knew she was in trouble. She then scurried over to the fence rail. She climbed through and exited the area. As she climbed on her horse and turned to ride out past the back side of the barn, one of the men came from around the barn and reeled at her horse. Her horse reared up and Katrina held on with all her might.

"Dear Lord, please help me," she prayed aloud.

As the horse came down on his front legs almost knocking the man over, the other man was there and reaching for the reins. Katrina kicked her heels into the horse's sides as hard as she dared to make him run. The horse practically knocked the man down as he started to sprint and as the other man was reaching for the reins, the horse threw his head into the man's arms. This knocked that man down to the ground. Katrina once again spurred her horse on and they raced across the pasture, but they weren't heading to the Whitaker Ranch. Katrina wasn't quite sure where her Uncle Tom and Jack were, but she knew she had to find them. She was hoping she was heading in the right direction.

Just as she entered the trail by the woods, she turned to see what was happening at the farm. She noticed the two men had mounted their horses and they were heading her way. Katrina turned back to the trail and rode as fast as she could get the horse to go. She prayed she wouldn't fall off.

It seemed like hours of riding hard. She wasn't sure which way she was going, but she could hear the horses behind her. She knew she couldn't stop. She rode through a field then picked up another trail at the edge of the field. She noticed the trail led along a rock fence that divided two fields that were filled with waist high wild weeds. Along the outer edge of the field she was riding in was a thick set of pines and the opposite side of another field had trees that were so big that you couldn't see any space between them. It was all bark and branches and leaves. She knew she couldn't ride through either set of woods so she continued at a fast pace on the trail. She noticed the trail took a right turn further up, she saw hills forming in the distance.

She decided to stay on the trail as she still heard the horses behind her. She didn't dare turn around to see how close they were. As the hills came nearer she noticed something to the side of one small hill. It appeared to be moving. The closer she got to the hill, the better she could see that there were two objects. She prayed again, *Dear Lord, please let it be someone I can trust.* The objects started to take shape. Yes, horses and someone on them. The closer these horses came to her, she realized she didn't hear the horses behind her. Once these men came into view, she felt a gentle breeze. She saw Uncle Tom and Jack. As they rode up to her, she tried to slow her horse down. Jack jumped off his horse and ran up to Katrina's horse to grab the reins and he was then able to stop the exhausted horse.

"Katrina, what's wrong? Are you all right?" shouted Uncle Tom.

Katrina was gasping for breath from her grueling ride and she then realized how scared she was. She responded back to Uncle Tom, "I'll be okay. But we need to get to the farm. There are men there. I heard them talking about cleaning the place out. They saw me and tried to catch me by the barn. Then they followed me. Didn't you see them chasing me?"

Jack was still holding the reins. He turned to Uncle Tom. "Take her back to the ranch and send some men to the farm. I'll meet them there." He turned back to Katrina, "Katrina, please go with your uncle." He handed the loose reins to Katrina.

She followed her uncle who wasn't wasting any time getting to the ranch. As they reached the ranch and she dismounted, she heard Uncle Tom talking to a bunch of the hands and next thing she knew, there was a cloud of dust as they rode off toward the farm.

Katrina was still breathing hard and as she walked toward the back door to the kitchen, she stopped by the water pump to splash water on her face. Then she entered the kitchen just as Mr. Whitaker was coming in from the hall. He noticed that Katrina looked bewildered so he asked her what was wrong. Katrina told him the story. Mr. Whitaker went out the back door towards the barn.

"Where's Pa going?" As he peered out the window toward the barn, Johnny watched his father mount a horse and ride away. "He didn't wait for me," exclaimed Johnny. He turned towards Katrina. "What's happening?" Katrina explained that they were checking some things out in one of the fields. She left it at that. Olivia was also in the kitchen during all of this. She pulled a fresh batch of molasses ginger cookies out of the oven. They happened to be Johnny's favorite kind and his attention was turned to the smell of those wonderfully scented sweet cookies in the bowl on the table.

Katrina went to her room to freshen up. She laid down on the bed just to catch her breath from the ordeal she had encountered. She fell asleep before she could say, 'Dear Lord'.

Katrina heard a knock on her bedroom door. She then realized she had fallen asleep. She heard the knock again. "Just a minute," she reported as she climbed off her bed. She looked quickly in the mirror and fixed her hair. Again, another knock, but this time louder. "I'm coming," she said as she crossed the room. When she opened the door, Jack was standing there.

"Hi! How are you after your episode?" asked Jack to Katrina with a very sincere worry.

"I'm fine now." Katrina entered the hallway and started down the stairs with Jack in tow.

"Did you get the men?"

"When I got to the farm they were in the house. I went around the house, peering in the windows watching them, waiting for Tom to show up. One of our ranch hands showed up and said your uncle went to town to get the sheriff." Jack and Katrina reached the bottom of the stairs. Jack took Katrina's arm and directed her to the parlor. "Come with me and I'll tell you more."

As they entered the parlor, Jack escorted her to the love seat and guided her to sit down as he sat next to her. Katrina looked around as if she was going to get up and sit somewhere else so they weren't sitting beside each other. She felt somewhat uncomfortable and then she realized she was blushing.

Jack continued his story. "Just about the time the intruders were ready to get out of the house, my father rode up, they noticed him ride up and went back into the house. He called them to come out of the house and put their hands up. Not sure what he was thinking."

All eyes and ears, Katrina was listening with much interest. She was so intent on listening to Jack that she hadn't realized he had his hand on her shoulder. Just the realization that his hand was on her body made her shiver with excitement. Jack thought she was chilled.

"Are you cold, Katrina?"

"No, not really," replied Katrina. "Go on, please keep going."

Jack never moved his hand. Katrina didn't let on that his hand touching her was the reason for the shiver.

Jack proceeded with the details of what took place at her uncle's farm.

"The men in the house started to laugh and I noticed one of them drew his gun out of his holster. I went quickly around to the side door and quietly let myself in the room. Before they knew I was there, my father had started to open the front door. When he had the door completely opened and his full body was standing there, the man with the gun took aim. I was then able to sneak up behind him and hit the gun out of his hand. At that time, two of his partners saw me and jumped on top of me, knocking me to the floor. My father was facing the man without the gun. That man struck my father. I was so angry that I didn't realize I had pushed both men off me and I lunged at the one who hit father."

Katrina gasped, "With all that, are you hurt?" as she gave him a quick once-over look.

"Naw," responded Jack, "I'm fine. I threw a punch at one and he tried to punch back just as Uncle Tom and the sheriff came into the house. They grabbed the one from behind as the other men from the posse grabbed the other two. They'll be in jail for a long time.

The sheriff found quite a few things in their packs and on the horses. They had a wagon full of items from your house and from other homes in the area. We won't be seeing them again."

Jack noticed Katrina's eyes sparkling. It made his heart feel funny. He thought, *Why does she make me feel this way?* He took his other hand and reached over for her hand lying in her lap. As he folded his fingers around her palm, he felt a tingle run through his fingers and up his arm. He gave a silent sigh. He didn't want her to know how she made him feel, but then he did want her to know. He wanted to shout to the world that he felt something special for her.

As Katrina felt his fingers in her hand she felt tingling run up her arm and throughout her body. She decided she liked this feeling. She didn't pull away. Without realizing it, she tightened her fingers around Jack's hand.

Jack felt the firmness of her hand. He knew she was pleased. Dare he go for a kiss? Hoping that no one entered the parlor, Jack decided to go for it. He leaned towards her. He felt the heat of emotions swell through his body as his face came closer to her face.

Katrina also felt the warmth from Jack. She liked the feeling and didn't want to pull away. Then their lips met. She lost herself and put her arms around Jack's neck. He in turn wrapped his arms around her and pulled her closer to him. After a couple of kisses, they heard some commotion near the doorway.

As they realized there was someone nearby, they released each other and straightened themselves out. As they both looked up at the same time, they saw Uncle Tom standing at the doorway looking at them.

"I've been standing here long enough to know what you two are up to," commented Uncle Tom.

"Uh, sir, I'm sorry." Before Jack could say anymore, Uncle Tom said, "No apologies. I was wondering how long it would be before you two found out that you're meant for each other."

"Uncle Tom!" exclaimed Katrina, "How would you know? What do you mean?"

"Katrina, do you take me for an old foggy? I was young once, too, ya know."

Katrina had the reddest face. Jack stood up and looked at Tom. "My apologies, sir. I didn't mean to take advantage. Yes, I'm in love with your niece. I hope and believe she feels the same for me." Jack turned to look at Katrina. She looked up with a smile but no words. Katrina rose and scurried out of the room.

Before Tom could turn and leave, Jack asked him to come in and have a seat. "I have to ask you something." Tom obliged and sat down in the single seat by the desk.

Jack turned towards Tom and walked over to his side. "Do you know why Katrina is asking about the church building?"

This question is not what Tom was expecting. It caught him off guard.

"What?" questioned Tom. "The church? What do you mean?"

"On the road, returning from town the other day, Katrina was asking about the church and what happened to it. Why it has been abandoned and why don't folks go to church?"

"I don't know," responded Tom. "She's never asked me about this."

Jack walked over to the window. "Tom, do you know anything about Katrina's past? Why did she come out here? Where did she come from?" Then he paused before continuing, "What made her come here?"

"Wow Jack. That's a lot of questions. Maybe you should ask her."

"I would but I don't want her to think I'm prying."

"Do you call that prying? I would call it wondering and caring about her," remarked Tom.

"Yes, I know," replied Jack. "I thought you might be able to give me some insight since she's your brother's daughter."

"Jack, I can tell you that my brother had a very personal life. When he left the family, he went east. He didn't keep in touch with any of us. I think Katrina is a lot like him; but, I wonder if she really doesn't want to be like her father. She seems to be reaching out to you and me. I say that because she hasn't left here considering all that has happened since she came here."

Tom then stood up. "Hang in there. Don't give up on her," he stated as he left the room.

Jack stood there. What Tom said made sense he thought.

Chapter 14

Several days had gone by. Things were quiet. Katrina had a routine day of getting up, eating breakfast with Lizzy, who's always so full of chatter and giggles. Johnny was up early and joined his father in riding out to check the fields and horses. There was a briskness in the air now and Katrina rode back to the farm to prepare the house for winter and to get the garden crops in before the first frost. Jack was just as consumed with the crops and animals now also. Everyone's paths seemed to be in passing.

One day, as Katrina awoke and dressed, she decided she wanted to go into town.

As she approached the dining room table she was surprised to see everyone was there already, eating. As she entered the room she took a plate from the buffet and put some fruit- orange slices and grapes, along with an oatmeal muffin on her plate. She sat at the only seat available at the table which happened to be next to Jack. She sat down and placed her cloth napkin on her lap, then reached for her fork. As she forked a grape Katrina inquired, "Is it possible for someone to take me into town today?"

"Yes, I can take you," replied Mr. Whitaker.

"Daddy, you promised me that we'd go to Mr. Tom's farm to help with the horses today," cried Johnny.

"Oh, yes I did, didn't I," snickered Mr. Whitaker. He took a sip of his coffee. "Katrina, I can't disappoint my boy."

"That's okay" replied Katrina. "I understand and I wouldn't expect you to renege on Johnny."

"Renege? What does that mean?" asked Johnny.

Mr. Whitaker replied, "It means take back. Don't worry, I promised you and we will go."

Mr. Whitaker reached over and gripped his son's shoulder then looked up at Jack as he stated, "Jack, you will have to take her." Mr. Whitaker then steered Johnny out of the room and Jack heard the back door close.

"Well, I guess I will be taking you to town today. When will you be ready?" asked Jack as he stood and pushed his chair in and walked over to Katrina and guided her chair away from the table as she pushed her chair back and stood. At that split second, she had reached for the back of the chair as Jack also put his hand on the back of the chair, their hands touched. Jack immediately put his hand on top and grasped her hand. She felt the tingling run through her hand, up her arm and directly to her heart. She gasped slightly and gave a shivering internal breath at the same time.

Jack also felt a shiver go up his arm and his heart skipped a beat.

They both looked into each other's eyes. Then Katrina knew the moment was special but awkward. She thought that anyone could walk in at any moment. She automatically looked toward the door.

Jack realized her discomfort when she looked toward the door so he removed his hand. She stepped away from the table and chair. Jack pushed her chair into the table as he commented. "I'll be ready to go in half an hour. Is that okay with you?"

"No problem, Jack," responded Katrina as she headed toward the door. "I'll meet you at the porch then." Katrina went to the kitchen. Jack headed out the back door.

As Katrina entered the kitchen, she reached for a basket on the shelf and placed it on the table in the center of the room. At that time, Olivia entered the room.

"Oh, Olivia, can you help me prepare a picnic lunch?" asked Katrina as she reached for a couple of apples from the bowl of fruit on the table.

"Sure can. What do you want to pack?" inquired Olivia.

Katrina responded, "What do we have that is quick to put together?"

"I can make some ham sandwiches," replied Olivia as she reached for a loaf of bread and began slicing it. "How about some cheese too?" asked Olivia.

"That will be great. Thanks, Olivia, for your help," remarked Katrina as she reached into the icebox and brought out a block of cheddar cheese and cut off a chunk and wrapped it in a cloth and placed it in the picnic basket. During that time, Olivia had three sandwiches made and wrapped in cloth. Olivia handed the sandwiches to Katrina who placed them in the basket making sure the apples didn't squash the fresh bread. Olivia threw in a couple of cloth napkins and closed the lid.

As Katrina took the handle of the basket to pick it up, Olivia threw her hands in the air, "Wait, I forgot the tablecloth!" Olivia went to a drawer and removed a folded cloth and placed it inside the basket and picked up the basket and handed it to Katrina with a wink in her eye as she giggled and turned away, still giggling once Katrina had the basket in hand.

Jack had the wagon ready to go. It was a fine summer day. The sun was shining with rays bouncing off the oak tree branches, leaves and the bright colored flowers. As Jack looked around, he was pleased with the weather.

Katrina walked out to the wagon. She noticed Jack looking around and then up at the sky. She wondered what he's looking at. She looked up and noticed the glorious sunshine blend through the air. *It looks beautiful today*, thought Katrina. "It's a beautiful day," she mentioned to Jack as she came closer to the wagon.

"Yes, it is," replied Jack as he reached for the picnic basket and touched her fingers as she handed it to him.

Katrina felt a soft warm breeze and a tingling all over her body. She looked up and in her mind thanked the Lord and her Dad for the wonderful weather. Jack assisted Katrina up to the seat and climbed beside her. He had already placed the basket under the seat to keep it in the shade. As they left the ranch, Jack was hoping to find out more about Katrina. He wasn't sure how to start the conversation.

"Jack," inquired Katrina, "please tell me more about the people in Widow's Peak." Katrina was gazing off in the distance.

Jack turned to look at Katrina while he snapped the reins encouraging the horses to continue down the roadway.

"What do you want to know? Folks that are there now or in the past?" asked Jack as he looked back toward the rump of the horses.

Katrina hesitated, then responded as she looked toward the front of the wagon. "I'd like to know it all. I figured since I'm going to be living at the farm. I should know the area which includes the town and the folks around. Doesn't that make sense?"

Jack thought, *She wants to stay.* As he turned to look at her again, he answered her, "Yes, that does make sense."

"I did tell you about how the town got its name, so now you want to know about folks who live there. Okay, where shall I start?" asked Jack as if he was asking himself.

"Let's start with the church . . ." stated Katrina.

"The church?" questioned Jack with a puzzled look on his face. "What's the infatuation with the church, Katrina?"

"I, I just was wondering since it sits empty. Doesn't anyone go to church here? I'm thinking there are no Christians in Widow's Peak," commented Katrina.

Jack again turned to look at Katrina, "Are you serious?" Jack smirked.

"What's funny?" asked Katrina as she turned to look at him.

"I'm confused, why do you wonder about Christians in Widow's Peak? What's going on with you, Katrina?" Jack became serious as he started to wonder what was really on her mind. She says she's staying. She's wondering about the church and the Christians in town. Suddenly, she decides she wants to find out about things. These things weren't on her mind before. What is going on with her?

Jack stopped the wagon on the trail. As he looked straight ahead he wanted to talk to her. He wanted answers like her, but he wanted them about her and her thoughts. He decided to answer her questions, then maybe she will answer his. He started the horses trotting again.

"Okay, the church has been empty since the pastor left. He left because his wife and children died after a very hard winter that we had. The pastor couldn't take it and went back east. No one was qualified to take over in the church. The town's people tried to get another pastor, but it seemed like there was no one who was interested in moving here. The other side of the story is that the church is haunted," exclaimed Jack.

Katrina gasped and with a puzzled look on her face, she remarked, "Haunted?!"

"Supposedly," replied Jack. "There was a gunfight many years ago and there were some bodies placed in the church. After that, folks started talking about the church being haunted."

"Like now," interjected Katrina.

"They say that there is a light that goes through the church at night. Folks have seen it go by the windows and they also hear noises inside the church when they walk by at night. It's very interesting," remarked Jack.

There was quiet for a few minutes with both concentrating on what's in front of them. At least it looked like that, as they were looking up the road in front of the horses. Katrina's thoughts were about the church. She wondered what the church would look like if it was cleaned up and had a congregation again.

Jack was wondering why Katrina had such an interest in the church. Just then, the town came into view and Jack asked Katrina where she wanted to go first. Katrina replied that she needed to go to the Post Office then the bank. Jack pulled the wagon up in front of the bank since the Post Office was nearby. Jack quickly jumped off and went in front of the horses to drape the reins over the hitching post and then he proceeded around to Katrina's side of the wagon to help her down.

Katrina entered the Post Office. Jack didn't follow her. He, instead, headed for the blacksmith's shop.

The Postmaster saw Katrina enter the room and he disappeared for a minute, then returned to the window. Katrina was standing at the window when the Postmaster returned.

"Miss Martin, I have a package for you as well as a letter. Please sign here for the package." The Postmaster turned a clipboard toward her and handed her a pen. As she took the pen, he tapped the paper where she was to sign. After she signed, he handed her both items and then asked her if there was anything else he could do for her. She thanked him and replied she was all set as she took her package and letter and went to a table in the middle of the room. She set down the package and opened the letter. It was from her lawyer back in Pennsylvania. She read the note to herself.

> *Katrina Martin, thank you for your inquiry about the investments of your Grandfather, Mr. Grant Henry. I have investigated the information you presented to me previously and have found that you are correct. Your Grandfather did leave you money from his investments. In my research, I discovered that your Mother had requested that the money be held until you requested it.*
>
> *I am pleased to tell you that since it has been several years since the money was set aside for you that you have significant interest accrued.*
>
> *Upon your request, I have kept twenty-five percent in your account and will forward the seventy-five percent that I have withdrawn. You shall receive a package along with the draft in the amount of $6,000.*

Just then, Jack walked up to Katrina and tapped her on the shoulder. "What a look you have on your face. Is everything okay?" inquired Jack.

Katrina practically jumped out of her skin and quickly thrust the letter into the envelope. "Jack, I'm not ready to go. I still need to go to the bank," stated Katrina as she grabbed the package and started toward the door.

"No problem," replied Jack. "I still have some things to do. I just stopped in to see if you wanted to grab some lunch while we're in town and save the picnic food for the trip back home."

"That won't be necessary," exclaimed Katrina, "We shouldn't be here long enough. The picnic basket will be lunch before we head back."

"That will work, too," responded Jack, trying not to show his disappointment.

Katrina was too involved with her own thoughts to notice Jacks' disappointed face.

"On to the bank," Katrina stated as she left and walked out the door. She quickly went to the bank and upon entering, noticed that Jack was gone. Now where did he go, she questioned to herself as she placed her package on the long table against the wall and proceeded to open it. She found the draft and placed the rest of the packaged items in her bag that she had brought with her. She walked over to the window and after signing it, handed it to the teller.

"Will this be a deposit or cash?" asked the teller.

"I would like to have this added to my savings, please," responded Katrina.

"Sure thing, ma'am." replied the teller as he stamped the check and wrote a receipt. He handed her the paper and said to Katina, "That's a nice nest egg. What do you plan to do with all that money?"

Katina didn't reply to the question. She took the receipt and thanked him as she turned away. Standing behind her was Jack.

"I'll be done in a minute here, Katrina." mentioned Jack as he walked up to the teller window.

Katrina wondered if he heard the remark from the teller about her savings, but she didn't want to bring it up just in case he didn't hear.

When Jack was done, he noticed Katrina walking out the door and he followed her. As they stepped out the door and onto the walkway, Jack took Katrina by the arm and turned her toward him. "Katrina, let's walk through town, I'll tell you more about it."

As Katrina looked up at Jack and saw into his eyes, she noticed true sincerity. Jack didn't have a mean look about him, not even a worried look. His demeanor was gentle and caring.

"I would love it, Jack," replied Katrina with a sweetness in her voice.

Jack still had a hold of her arm. He noticed she didn't pull away so he continued to hold her arm as they walked. Katrina realized that she never really paid much attention to town. She remembered the day she arrived. It seemed so long ago but it really wasn't.

As they approached Wally's General Store, Jack stopped by the door and turned to Katrina. "Need anything in here? Do you want to go in?" asked Jack.

Katrina had not been to a mercantile in ages and since they were here in town, she decided to be adventurous. "Sure, I haven't been in a mercantile since I came here," stated Katrina. They entered and Jack stayed by Katrina's side as they walked and stopped to look at items. Jack was watching Katrina's eyes as he noticed the gleam in her eyes when she saw a small trinket box adorned with gold trim. The lid opened and the box played music. Jack knew he had heard the music before, but couldn't remember the name of the waltz. Katrina was smiling as she held the box up in the light. Jack thought for sure she would take it to buy, but she put it down and continued to browse down the aisle.

As they finished their walk around the store and started to head out the door, they had to wait for people to come in. After the way through the door was clear, Jack motioned for Katrina to go through first, then he followed her. Just as he stepped over the threshold, there was a familiar face approaching him. It was Constance. He knew he had to say something since he was brought up with manners. Jack tipped his hat and stepped aside at the same time he said, "Constance" with a matter of fact tone and put his hand on Katrina's back as a sign to keep moving. He wanted to avoid further communication with Constance. As Jack and Katrina stepped off the boardwalk to cross the street, he heard a voice behind him.

"Jack, is that all you're going to say?" remarked Constance as she turned to watch him and Katrina walk away.

"Sorry, we have an appointment to keep," stammered Jack. Katrina looked quickly at Jack and then at Constance. She sensed that Jack was uncomfortable and attempting to avoid communication with this lady. Katrina took the cue and put her hand on his arm, "Jack, we'll be late." Then she turned to look at Constance and stated, "Good day!"

Jack realized that Katrina knew his situation and was helping. He continued walking with his hand on Katrina's back. He whispered to Katrina, "Thanks." She whispered back, "You're welcome."

They walked by the doctor's office and came up to the dress shop. Katrina walked slower to see the dresses in the window. She saw a beautiful, off the shoulder, full skirted blue shimmering dress. She thought about how exquisite it looked and gave a quick thought about how it would look on her. She suddenly realized she stopped. She became flushed in the face and started to walk along hoping Jack wasn't paying attention.

Jack noticed Katrina's hesitation in front of the dress shop and saw that she was looking at the blue dress in the window. He thought, how beautiful she would look in that dress. He was still looking at the dress as he realized Katrina was a few steps ahead of him. Without looking around, Jack caught up with Katrina.

They walked a few more steps together when Katrina stopped in front of the church. She stood looking at the abandoned building. Her face showed a sadness. Jack noticed her emotional distress. He put his arm around Katrina's back and shoulders and squared her off in front of him. "What's the matter, Katrina?" He thought quickly to himself, Was she upset because of Constance?

Katrina looked in Jack's face and answered him. "Jack, it just breaks my heart to see the House of the Lord sit there looking so forlorn and lonely. It's unfortunate that the folks in this town let this happen."

Jack looked at the building in front of him. He also saw an empty, forlorn structure. As Jack was trying to recall what happened, his attention was then focused on Katrina standing at the top of the sixth step. Before he could call out to her, Katrina took another step and her foot went through the floorboard. She reached for the railing of the porch and it leaned away from her. Jack ran up the steps and reached for Katrina, just as she was halfway down to the floor. He managed to keep her from falling and then pulled her to his chest as he righted her.

"Are you all right?" shouted Jack in a state of panic.

"I'm, I'm fine, thank you." Katrina looked up to Jack's face. She saw that he had a genuine concern for her. As she looked straight into his caring eyes, Jack stood her on her feet and guided her back down the steps. At that time, Katrina noticed there were several folks running their way.

In all the commotion, folks were running up and asking if they were alright.

Jack responded, "She will be. Thanks for your concern." Jack turned to Katrina. "Let's get your foot checked out."

Katrina looked around and then at Jack, "I am okay." She brushed her skirt off and stood up straight to walk.

He noticed she was limping and not putting pressure on her leg. "I think you did get hurt. I'm taking you to the doctor." He went to her other side and put his arm around her waist and helped her walk down the street. As they entered the doctor's office, there were a couple of folks in the sitting room.

Katrina then said to Jack, "I'm fine. There are others who need the doctor more than me." She tried to turn around to go back out the door.

"Oh, no. You are getting checked out by the doctor," remarked Jack as he placed his arm around her waist.

Just then the doctor came out of a room guiding an elderly man out the door. "I'll see you in a couple days," stated the doctor. As the doctor released his hold on the man, he looked up and noticed Jack holding Katrina.

"What has happened here?" inquired the doctor.

"Doc Abrams, this is Katrina Martin. She tried to go into the old church and her foot went through the rotten boards at the top of the steps. Can you check out her foot and leg, please?"

"Bring her in here," stated the doctor as he stepped aside to allow Jack to escort Katrina into the room.

"Need her on the table," stated Dr. Abrams.

Jack picked up Katrina and sat her on the table. She felt the warmth of his hands around her waist. She put her hands on his shoulders to balance herself. While the doctor grabbed a wash basin and poured water in it, he asked to have her shoe and stockings be removed. Jack reached for Katrina's foot and started to unlace the shoe. Katrina felt uncomfortable and reached for his hand as she replied, "I can manage, thank you."

"Oh," stammered Jack. "Of course, you can. I'll step out to the waiting room," stated Jack as he departed from the room.

"Now," exclaimed the doctor, "tell me what happened?" He reached for her shoe and removed it. "It appears that you scraped your leg and your foot is swollen. Your stocking is torn so I'm going to cut it and remove it from just above the ankle so I can get to the cuts, as small as they are, you can never be too careful. It doesn't take much to acquire an infection." The doctor cleaned the wounds and wrapped the lower leg, ankle and foot. Once he finished, he went to the door and motioned for Jack to come in.

"Jack, please take this young lady home. She needs to get her feet up for a couple of days. The wrap should be changed tomorrow. If the swelling doesn't go down, send for me. Understand?" The doc was looking at Jack.

"Excuse me, Doctor Abrams, I am right here and am capable of taking care of myself," exclaimed Katrina.

"Oh, yes, dear, I'm sorry, but someone will need to insure you stay off your leg for a while," stated the doctor.

Jack had left the doctor's office to get the wagon. He drove it up to the walk and then went in to help Katrina get up in the seat of the wagon. Then he climbed up and sat next to her.

"Where to now? Are you done here in town?" asked Jack as he looked down to her sore foot.

"I did have a couple other things I wanted to do, but, it will have to wait now," replied Katrina as she reached down with her hand to rub her leg.

"You need to get that foot up, so let's get home."

As Jack drove out of town, the wind picked up and clouds started to form in the northern sky. The further they drove, the darker the sky became. Jack was hurrying the horses. As they reached Widow's Peak, Jack knew they wouldn't be able to outrun the storm.

"I'm heading to the farm. We'll never make the ranch," exclaimed Jack as he urged the horses on at a faster clip.

Just as the farm house came into sight, it started raining slightly. By the time they reached the front of the house, it was pouring and lightening was flickering all around them.

Jack stopped the wagon as near to the porch as he could get. He jumped off and ran around to Katrina's side as she tried to stand.

Her foot slipped on the wet floorboard. Jack reached up to catch her and lifted her out of the wagon and carried her to the door. Katrina leaned over to open the door and they entered the room. Jack sat her on a chair and said, "I'll be right back. Gonna' get the horses in the barn." He reached over to a drying rack by the fireplace and pulled a blanket off and wrapped it around Katrina.

"Don't move from there," shouted Jack as he went out the door. It seemed like an eternity before Jack returned. Although he didn't waste any time in getting the horses unhitched from the wagon and into stalls in the barn. He rubbed them down quickly so they didn't get a chill. He gave them some grain and water, then left them.

He half expected Katrina to be out of the chair when he walked back into the house. He was surprised to see her still sitting there. She was wrapped tightly with the blanket and looked pale.

"Katrina, are you all right?" asked Jack as he went to her side and rubbed her shoulders. "Are you cold?"

"I'll be fine," replied Katrina.

"Let me fix you some tea and get the fire going."

Jack went to the fireplace and started a fire then filled the tea kettle to put over the flames to heat the water. He went to find the tin of tea and put some in a tea bag.

"While we're waiting for the water to get hot, let's get you comfortable." Jack went into the adjoining room, then came back out. As he went to Katrina, he noticed she was shaking. "Okay, we're going to get you to bed." Jack picked her up and carried her to the bedroom and sat her on the bed.

"Katrina, you need to take your wet clothing off. I'll step out so you can. Let me know when you need help." Jack walked out of the room.

Katrina unbuttoned her dress top and removed it down to her waist, then scooted back to the head of the bed, where Jack had already pulled the covers down. She was then able to move herself out of the rest of the dress. She kicked her dress to the floor. She then set herself in a sitting position and pulled the covers up.

"All set, Jack."

Jack came in with her cup of tea. He was surprised to see her already under the covers. As he handed her the teacup, he noticed her wet dress on the floor and picked it up. "I'll hang this by the fire to dry." Jack took the dress and left the room. Katrina took a sip of the tea. It was hot, but felt it warm her throat. She took another sip. Jack returned with a plate of bread and cheese.

"Are you by chance hungry?"

"A little," replied Katrina.

He set the plate on the bed next to Katrina and then sat on the edge of the bed and commented, "It's a good thing you brought the picnic basket." Then with a thoughtful look he continued, "Katrina, we'll have to spend the night. The storm will be over, come the morning, then we can get back to the ranch."

"Okay," said Katrina after a slight hesitation.

"Are you okay, Katrina? You're very quiet," inquired Jack.

"Jack?"

"Yes, Katrina."

"I'm still cold," commented Katrina. She handed him the empty teacup and took a piece of cheese. Jack also took a piece of cheese and put it in his mouth.

He wondered if she would object if he laid next to her. He knew that body heat would get her warm, but he didn't want to offend her. He looked at her lying there. He noticed that she was still shaking. He left the room for a minute, then returned with a stoneware hot water bottle and placed it under the blankets near her feet.

"Maybe this will help you." said Jack after placing the bottle under the blankets.

"Jack, you'd better get out of your wet clothes and get warm too, before you catch your death of a cold," murmured Katrina, as she looked up at his face and noticed how soaked he was - wet hair and all.

"Ya, I'd better. I'll be out in the other room. Call if you need me," remarked Jack as he walked out of the room.

Jack stripped down to his long johns and hung his clothing to dry. He found a towel and dried his hair. Before he could sit down, he heard Katrina moaning. He went to the bedroom door and looked in. "Are you okay?" he asked.

Katrina turned toward the door, "Jack, I hate to ask this, but would you mind staying in here?"

Jack looked around the room. "I'll bring a chair in."

"No, I need you in bed to keep me warm. I don't, can't get warm for some reason and I know they say heat from another body helps. I can't stop shivering. Please?" begged Katrina.

"Are you sure?" asked Jack.

Katrina patted the space beside her. Jack sat on the bed and looked at her. "It's okay," stated Katrina.

Jack went to lay on top of the covers. He started to put his feet on the blanket.

"You might want to get under the covers so you can stay warm. Won't do me any good getting body heat with you on top of the covers," she replied. Without further conversation, Jack took off his boots and moved the covers over himself as he got more comfortable. He wasn't sure which way to lay, facing her or with his back to her.

He decided to lay on his back. While lying next to Katrina, Jack's mind was so mixed up with thoughts. He wondered what would happen. How would she react if he ended up with his arm around her come morning? What if someone came in and found them together in bed? He thought about a few other wonderful things, *Is this what it's like to have a wife?*

On a winter night, this would be the best way to keep warm, in the arms of a wonderful lady. Then he had thoughts that made him anxious and nervous. Or is this what it's like to get a reputation if they are found like this? What if he gets excited from being so close to her and they end up being real close during the night. *Stop thinking like this. Don't make it out to be more than it is. It is an innocent situation. Isn't it?* he questioned himself, then decided he could pray on it. "Lord, guide me to be the perfect gentleman."

Katrina was so cold and tired, she never gave it a thought that this situation was not proper. She didn't want to get sick. She wanted to be warm. So, she prayed, "Lord, help me to feel better and get warm. Thank you for Jack being here. He is such a gentleman. I know I can trust him. Thank you for Jack." She drifted off to sleep. Jack looked over and noticed that Katrina was sleeping. Okay, he thought. She must be comfortable to be asleep already. I need to get some sleep, too. Jack was soon asleep.

Daylight peered into the room. Katrina woke to find she had her arm draped over Jack's chest as he laid sleeping on his back. And Jack had his hand on her arm. She smiled as she noticed this and quickly looked up to see if he was awake. His eyes were closed. She tried to remove her arm from the hold, but Jack had a firm grip. She thought maybe he's not sleeping. A person is usually relaxed when asleep. Katrina left her arm on his chest. She felt this position was comfortable, relaxing. It seemed right, then she thought, am I ready for this? Is Jack ready for this? She closed her eyes and before she knew it, she drifted off to sleep again.

When Katrina woke the second time, Jack was still beside her, but he was awake. "Morning, sleepyhead!"

Katrina replied, "Good morning."

"Yes, it is," smirked Jack as he looked at her and smiled. "How are you feeling?" inquired Jack.

"Great," replied Katrina. "My leg feels better. I should be able to get around today."

"We'll head back to the ranch after breakfast. How about I find us something to eat. I'll see what there is to eat."

"Or, we can just catch breakfast at the ranch if we get going," suggested Katrina.

"We could. It's up to you."

"Well, you go get the horses ready," replied Katrina as she started to crawl out of the covers. Then she held the covers and recovered herself. Jack got out of bed as Katrina closed her eyes. He left the room to get his clothes then he brought her dress in so she could get dressed.

Jack got the wagon together and brought it up to the house. The sun was shining bright and there were no clouds in the sky. But, he noticed the rain and wind left some damage to the barn and porch. Trees were down near the fence line. He knew there was work to be done.

As he entered the main room, Katrina was by the fireplace folding the blanket that she had used the night before. She took it in the bedroom and returned. Jack saw a slight limp, but felt she was better than she was last night.

"Not cold anymore?" Jack winked.

"Nope." replied Katrina with a smile.

As Jack helped her up onto the wagon seat, he mentioned having to come back to do the repairs that the storm had caused.

Katrina looked at him with pleading eyes, "I'd like to come back, too."

"Are you sure?" asked Jack.

"Jack, this farm is why I came out here. I care about Lizzy and enjoy taking care of things for Mr. Whitaker, but that's not where I want to be. At least not at this stage of my life."

Jack knew that Katrina felt better, she was talking again. "I understand," he stated as he encouraged the horses to head home.

"Jack?" inquired Katrina.

"Yes!" responded Jack.

"Thank you for taking care of me last night." This sounded like such a kind, caring statement. Jack replied, "You are welcome. To be honest I was happy to be there for you." Jack smiled as he said that and Katrina saw a sweetness in him that made her heart flutter. A soft, gentle breeze blew by them and at the same time, Jack said, "Your father," as Katrina answered, "yes, my father." They both laughed. They knew it was a sign. Then there was silence as they both were deep in thought about what happened last night.

Chapter 15

Back at the ranch, breakfast was already over, but they found some muffins as they entered the kitchen. Amelia put the teakettle on and poured Jack a cup of coffee.

Mr. Whitaker came into the kitchen. "I see you managed to survive the storm. Did you stay in town?"

Jack made a matter of fact statement as he took a sip of his coffee. "No, at the farm, we were drenched by the time we got there." He didn't offer any other information. Katrina was eating her muffin and Amelia set her cup of tea in front of her.

"Oh, I see," replied Mr. Whitaker.

Jack finished his muffin and downed a cup of coffee when he stood up and left the room heading out to the barn.

Before Katrina could finish her tea, in bounded Lizzy. "Oh Katrina! You are home. I missed you last night. I thought you'd be home for supper," cried Lizzy.

"I would have been if it wasn't for the storm."

Lizzy gave Katrina a hug and then said see you later as she skipped out of the room and went outside.

Amelia had disappeared. Katrina made her way up the stairs and to her room to clean up and change. Her leg was swelling again. She decided to lay down for a little while to get her feet up and stop the swelling.

It was heading toward noon so Jack went in to grab something to eat. Amelia was in the kitchen feeding Johnny and Lizzy.

Jack inquired where Katrina was. Johnny shrugged his shoulders. Lizzy said don't know with food in her mouth. Amelia reprimanded her for doing so, then looked at Jack. "I haven't seen her since you two came in this morning."

Jack left the kitchen and ran up the stairs. He knocked, but got no answer. He didn't hesitate. He opened the door to find her in bed, sleeping. Jack went to her bedside to see if she was feverish. He felt her forehead with the back of his hand. She didn't feel like she had a fever. Katrina opened her eyes and looked up at him.

"I'm all right," she whispered. "I laid down because my leg was swollen." Katrina removed the covers and sat up to look at her leg. Jack looked also. The swelling was gone.

"Good, it's better. Now I can get up," Katrina remarked.

"No, you're not. Please stay down today to ensure your leg is better," requested Jack.

"But, I have things to do," begged Katrina.

"I'll tell you what. If you stay down today, I'll take you to the farm tomorrow. I know you'd rather be there. So, I will let my father and your uncle know that you want to be at the farm, living there.

Katrina quickly looked up at Jack, "Really? Oh, Jack, yes, that's what I want. Thank you." Katrina raised her left hand to her eye and wiped a tear and turned to her side. Jack walked out of the room.

Jack had to think about how he was going to be able to convince Tom to allow Katrina to stay at the farm. Would Tom let her stay there by herself? Should she be there alone? Jack knew he wanted to be there with her but knew it wouldn't be appropriate. He decided to think about it and address the situation tomorrow. Jack went back outside to the barn.

Tom was in the barn when Jack entered carrying a pail. Jack noticed Tom brushing down a brown mare. He thought maybe this was the right time. He knew it was just the two of them in the barn and decided, it's now or never.

"Hi, Tom. How are you today?" asked Jack as he put the pail on the bench near the stall where Tom was standing.

Tom turned towards Jack. "Hi, doing good and you?" replied Tom as he continued brushing the mare.

"Tom, I need to talk to you. Do you have a minute?" inquired Jack as he went and stood next to Tom.

Tom stopped brushing and turned toward Jack. "What's on your mind, son?"

"Well, Katrina has mentioned that she misses the farm. Do you think she could go stay there again?"

"Well, I would love it if she was back at the farm, but not alone?" remarked Tom. "There are ranch hands working there. They will have to stay in the barn if she's in the house. But, even then, I'm not comfortable having her alone there. I would have to go back and stay with her. I wouldn't mind doing that," commented Tom as he went back to brushing the mare.

Jack replied, "Well, why can't you? Go back to stay there that is."

"That would be up to your father," winked Tom as he turned back to Jack.

"Now that father is settled from mother's death, he should be able to go back to running the ranch. That would free you up to go back to the farm then," stated Jack. "And, Katrina can go back to the farm if you can go back, right?" asked Jack.

"Jack, why are you asking this? Is Katrina all right?" asked Tom with a puzzled, concerned look on his face.

"Well," exclaimed Jack as he ran his hand through his hair. "Katrina was mentioning this. She... I think she has something on her mind."

"What makes you say that?" questioned Tom.

"Well, she's been asking questions about folks in town, the church and other things. When I've taken her to town, she goes to the Post Office every time, then the bank. Except this last time, she wanted to walk around town. Until we ran into Constance. I wasn't sure about things." Jack's eyes stared off to the doorway.

"And what are you sure of now, Jack." inquired Tom.

"Tom, I, I . . . think, I'm in love with Katrina," replied Jack as he looked directly at Tom.

"Well," replied Tom. "It's about time you confessed it."

"What?" asked Jack with a surprised look.

Tom went to Jack and had him sit down on the bench. "Jack, I've known for quite some time that there are sparks between the two of you. Just wondered how long it would take the two of you to find out. I'll talk to your father about releasing me so I can go back home and that I will need Katrina to go, too. I'm going out to the south pasture with him today." Tom put the horse brush on the shelf and left the barn.

Jack remained sitting on the bench. *I confessed my feelings to Tom, again,* he thought. *Oh, no, I didn't ask Tom to not let anyone know! What if Tom says something to father?* wondered Jack. Jack was nervous now. He left the barn and walked around to the back. He called for his horse who came running once he heard Jack's voice. Jack saddled him and rode off toward the farm. Jack tried to not think about things. He wanted to clear his head. He couldn't understand why this bothered him so much.

Just as he came in view of the farm, he felt a gust of wind. It was only once, then gone. He thought, *Could Katrina's father be giving me a sign?* Was it him or was he imagining things. Was this what Katrina felt? Jack started thinking about all the times he was with Matt, Katrina's father. John taught Jack how to rope a calf. He taught Jack how to fish. Jack then thought about how busy his own father was. His Pa never had time for him, but Matt made time for him.

Jack approached the house and dismounted his horse and tied him up at the railing. He went up on the porch and sat on the bench, looking out over the pasture.

I can understand why Katrina wants to be here, he thought. *I feel the same way. But, if anyone should be here, it should be Katrina. She came out here from . . . did she say Pennsylvania?* Jack wondered what made her decide to come out here. Why now? He realized that there's so much he doesn't know about Katrina. He had questions about her. But he knew he couldn't ask her such questions. How could he find out about her? He wanted to know more about her. The more he thought about things, the more he was curious. Jack suddenly realized that he had to stop this. It was going to drive him crazy. He stood up and went inside and made some coffee.

Jack walked around looking at everything in the main room while drinking his coffee. Before he knew it, it was turning dark. Jack decided to stay the night. He went out to take care of his horse and returned shortly. Jack decided to turn in and get a good night's sleep then head back to the ranch early in the morning.

At dinner, everyone wondered where Jack was. Tom mentioned seeing him ride off toward the farm.

Katrina wondered why Jack went to the farm. While she was thinking of things Jack could be doing at the farm, Johnny spoke up saying Jack had been acting strange the past couple of days. Mr. Whitaker glanced toward Katrina then at Tom. He asked if anyone knew what Jack was up to. No one knew.

Lizzie remarked after a moment of silence. "Poppa, there's a dance in town this Saturday. Can we go?"

Mr. Whitaker looked at his beautiful little girl and replied, "I believe the dance is for older folks."

Lizzie commented, "There's nothing for those my age to do here in town. It is not fair!" She exclaimed further, "Wish I could do something fun with my friends. We never get to spend time together."

Katrina thought about the things she did when she was younger. The games, the picnics and dances in town, at the church, at school. This got her to thinking more about the town and the abandoned church. She wanted to talk about it, but wasn't sure who could help her.

Katrina laid in bed that night wondering what she should do. If she should talk to Uncle Tom, Mr. Whitaker, or Jack? Who would understand her the most? There was no pastor to talk to, a town mayor or a sheriff? She had been here for quite a while and didn't know much about the people in town. She thought about when she was in Pennsylvania. But she knew that that's a chapter of her life she wanted to leave behind, in the past, where it should stay.

Katrina resolved to the fact that she had to talk to someone. She figured she would start with Uncle Tom. She decided to find him and set up a time to have a talk. Katrina drifted off to sleep.

When morning came, she jumped out of bed and dressed, then she went downstairs but no one was to be found in any of the rooms. She stepped out the back door and glanced toward the barn. Still, she didn't see anyone around. She went back inside the kitchen. Just as she went to the table in the center of the room, Amelia entered through the door that led to the dining room.

"Amelia, I was looking all over for someone. Where is everyone?" asked Katrina.

Amelia stopped in her tracks and stared at Katrina. "Don't you know?" questioned Amelia as she started toward the stove. "They all went to town this morning."

"Oh, well, thank you, Amelia." Katrina started to head back out to the barn. As she opened the door she turned to Amelia. "I'm going for a ride today. Not sure when I'll be returning. Just in case anyone is looking for me."

Katrina saddled up a horse and rode toward the farm. She wanted to be at the farm today. After all, that was her home and she was feeling lost, without a connection to anything or anyone right now.

As she approached the farmhouse, she noticed the weeds in the garden and flower beds. She realized that the farmhouse had been neglected. *Well,* she thought, *this is a good time to put my energy to good use.*

She put the horse in the pasture and the saddle on the fence rail. As she walked up to the porch she pulled a few weeds from the side of the steps and tossed them in a pile. "First, I'll get a drink then start on the weeds near the porch," she said to herself.

As she entered the house she smelled the coffee and saw a pot on the stove. The fire in the stove was pretty burned down, but obviously, someone had been here. She shouted out to find out if anyone was inside. No answer back. Then she wondered if Uncle Tom had been here. She forgot that Jack mentioned going to the farm.

She drew water from the pump into a glass and drank it. She went to the small table by the window and found a pair of work gloves that she put on and then went outside. After spending about an hour tending to the weeds, she had the flowerbed finished.

The clouds started filling in the sky and it was getting darker. Off in the distance she heard thunder. She surmised that a storm was brewing and with the way the sky was looking, she decided she better stay at the farm for a while. She went inside to find some food as she didn't have any breakfast and she was sure it was well into the afternoon. She found some potatoes and onions. There was a tin of lard on the shelf. She pulled out the cast iron pan, cut up the potatoes and onions and threw them in the pan with a spoonful of lard. Fried potatoes and onion aroma started to fill the air. She gave it a stir and went to start a fire in the fireplace to help keep the chill out of the air as the evenings were starting to get cooler. Katrina went over to stir supper again just as the door opened and Jack entered the room.

"Katrina, what are you doing here?" inquired Jack.

"I wanted to do something different today. No one was at the ranch, so I came here," responded Katrina.

"You won't be able to go back to the ranch for a while. There's a bad storm brewing in the distance and it's coming in fast." Just then there was a clap of thunder and they saw lightning flash by the window.

"Looks like it'll be a doozy of a storm! Glad I'm inside," commented Katrina.

"Smells good in here. Is there enough for me, too?" asked Jack.

"Sure, I can share," winked Katrina. "Want some heated up coffee? Is this yours from earlier today?"

"Yes," stated Jack. "It's mine from earlier, but I'd rather have a cup of tea. Will you have one, too? Tea, that is."

"Sounds good," said Katrina as she reached for the tea kettle.

"I'll fill it," remarked Jack as he took the kettle from her and went to the pump. He returned the filled kettle to the stove and stood behind Katrina as she stirred the potatoes.

"Smells great. Interesting how something so simple can make such a great meal." Jack went to the shelf and took two plates and set the table. By the time the teakettle was steaming, Jack had the cups and tea ready for the water. While he poured the water, Katrina dished out the supper and they both sat down to eat.

Katrina bowed her head and gave a silent prayer. Jack noticed and did the same. *Thanks Lord for bringing Katrina to me.* They ate in silence while the thunder raged in the distance and flashes of light seemed to get brighter and closer.

After finishing her supper, Katrina looked at Jack, "Can we talk?"

"Sure, are you okay, Katrina?" inquired Jack. He looked in to her beautiful blue eyes.

"What do you want to talk about?"

"Jack, you know I've asked about the church and other things?" She hesitated then as she pushed her plate away and moved her tea-cup closer, she continued. "I have been confused, feeling out of sorts, haven't had anyone to talk to in a long time." She drew a breath and noticed that Jack was listening. "I have been feeling lonely." She stopped talking, trying to sort things out in her mind.

Jack got up and moved to a chair that was closer to her. As he sat, he reached for her hand to hold it.

"I'm listening," he said.

"I . . . I don't know where to start and how much to tell you. I had thought I would talk about this with Uncle Tom, but I haven't seen him in a while and I've been feeling kind of like I'm having panic attacks. I don't like how I've been feeling lately."

"I'm listening, go on." pleaded Jack.

"I came here from Pennsylvania because I had no one there. After my mother died, I tried to stay in the house but couldn't keep up the finances and maintenance. I worked several jobs but I was so lost that I started to not show up. I slept a lot. I was depressed. So, I decided to leave and make a new start elsewhere. I remembered mother saying that father lived in a town out west. I found some papers that had information about my father and Uncle Tom. So, I sold the house and furniture and took a train out to Widow's Peak. So here I am. I still feel like I'm searching for something. When I saw the church, I realized that I was missing my faith."

"And a place to call home, right?" added Jack. "I know about that."

Katrina suddenly realized she wasn't alone in her feelings.

"Jack, you're lost, too?" asked Katrina.

Jack let go of her hand and leaned back in his chair. "I guess you could say that."

Katrina looked off to the fireplace that was starting to die down. Jack noticed what she was looking at and got up and went to restock the fire. While he did that, Katrina got up and collected the dirty dishes and pulled the pot of boiling water off the wood stove that she put there while supper was cooking. She washed the dishes and

Jack came over to dry them. Once the dishes were done, Jack poured more hot water for their tea cups and they sat back at the table.

"I would like to hear more, Katrina. What about the church?" Jack once again took her hand to hold.

Katrina didn't know if she was comfortable with him holding her hand. She started to pull her hand away as Jack took a firmer hold. She didn't want to create any problems so she left her hand where it was. She knew deep down that she felt a warm feeling in her heart and a tingling in her stomach. She had to concentrate on something so she wasn't noticing the strange, yet exciting feeling. Okay, talk about the church so you can get your mind off this wonderful feeling, she said to herself as she took her other hand to pick up her cup to drink from it to wet her mouth before she started talking.

"The church, it sits there empty. Don't folks go to church?" asked Katrina, after setting her cup down and keeping her fingers on the cup.

Jack replied, "I . . . well, I guess they pray in their homes. Folks used to a long time ago." Jack removed his hand from Katrina's and took a drink from his cup. Katrina quickly moved her hand and placed both of her hands in her lap.

Jack continued talking. "I remember some as a little boy going to church and that there was a picnic afterwards with lots of food and games and singing. But, I don't remember much as I got older, because my father stopped going." Jack had been looking across the room as he talked. When he stopped talking he looked directly at Katrina. "There was something about a man who came to town, I think."

"But, you don't remember what happened?" asked Katrina.

"It was so long ago. I think I was about six or seven years old. I seem to remember my father was very angry. I wonder if it had to do with my mother leaving.

It was about that same time," mentioned Jack.

"She left?" inquired Katrina with a surprised look. "Do you mean she moved away or passed away?"

Jack made a puzzled look on his face. "I think she left. I never gave it much thought. Father kept me busy on the ranch."

Katrina noticed that Jack was becoming upset. She decided to change the subject. "It is getting late. I guess I should turn in." Katrina stood and picked up the cups and put them in the dishpan. She saw Jack get up and head towards the door. "I'll put the horses to bed and bring in some more wood," said Jack as a clap of thunder was heard.

"Guess it's still storming. I forgot about it while we were talking. I'll be back soon." Jack left.

Katrina heard the wind pick up. It was quite strong. She silently prayed for Jack to be safe and return soon as she went to the bedroom to get ready for bed.

It wasn't long before she heard the front door close. She looked up toward the sky and whispered, "thank you." She felt a comfort as she knew talking to the Lord again was good. It had been a long time and she was realizing how much she had missed it and needed it.

Then she remembered that she never really answered Jack about the church.

Katrina put on her robe that was hanging on a peg on the wall and went out to the main room. Jack was putting a couple of logs on the fire. When he heard her open the door and come out of the bedroom, he turned to look at her. He suddenly realized that the situation felt real and wonderful. Then he wondered if this is what it would be like if they were husband and wife.

Katrina went over and sat in the rocking chair. Jack sat in the overstuffed chair that was next to the small stand which was in between him and the rocker.

"Jack?" asked Katrina with a puzzled look on her face while she played with the tie on the robe. She didn't wait for an answer from Jack. "I have some money. I'd like to rebuild the church. Do you think folks will want to go to church if it was functional again?"

This time she waited for an answer.

Jack looked at Katrina then to the fireplace and he paused for a minute. As he turned his head back to Katrina, he had a concerned look on his face. "Katrina, I honestly don't know, maybe, just maybe, if the church was rebuilt and some folks started to go, after a while the others may start to go. But, what about a preacher?"

"Well, there are seminaries where young men are trained to preach. Maybe we could send for someone who has graduated. Or a retired pastor who wants to be back at the pulpit. Could put an ad in the paper for someone. Or is there someone in Widow's Peak who would like to preach the word of the gospel?"

Jack responded, "You have apparently been thinking, after rattling off those options."

"I have been thinking," she paused. "Jack, do you think it's possible?"

"Yes, I do. I also think that it will take a lot of work and a lot of prayers."

Katrina looked up at Jack and burst out laughing and replied, "You believe in prayers?"

Then she turned serious, "Will you pray with me now?" She looked at Jack's face trying to read his emotion about praying.

Jack's face turned serious. "I'm not good at praying. Will you show me how to pray?"

Katrina stood up and went in front of Jack and she knelt-down on her knees. "Jack, put your hands together, close your eyes and talk to the Lord as you would a friend. Say what's in your heart."

Katrina took Jack's hands and pressed them together. They both closed their eyes.

Jack didn't say anything. Katrina sensed his anxiety so she started to pray.

"Lord, I have someone here who wants to talk to you. As you can see, he is nervous and a new believer, I hope. Please guide his mind and heart so he can say the words of how he feels. And dear Lord, thank you for being a part of this day and now this special time. My love for you was lost, but now I pray to you to please forgive me for my absence. I have found you again.

"Lord, I pray that you will open your arms for Jack. Please let him feel the peace you bring. In Jesus' name, Amen."

She opened her eyes and looked at Jack. He had his eyes closed.

"Go ahead Jack, your turn," said Katrina as she let go of his hands and sat back on her haunches.

Jack hesitated, then he started to speak, slowly, "Dear Lord, I too, have been away from you. It has been so long, I . . . I almost forgot about you. But, thankfully, this young lady has brought it back to the forefront of my mind. I know, dear Lord, that you are the alpha and omega. I realize what I've been missing, a part that I have felt lost with, in a long time. Father, I need you now.

"Please accept my request for forgiveness. And know that I do love you. I pray that you allow me to be back in your embrace. Thank you, Lord, in the name of Jesus Christ."

Jack raised his head and opened his eyes. He saw that Katrina had her eyes closed and she whispered, "Amen." She stood up at the same time Jack got out of the chair and was standing in front of her. He looked directly into her face and smiled. He reached over and gave her a hug as he whispered in her ear, "Thank you, Katrina, I needed that. You helped me to find the one thing I've been missing for so long. And I didn't realize it 'til now. Once I started, the words just flowed."

Katrina stood there with her arms down to her side. Jack still had his arms around her. He searched her eyes once again as he softly spoke to her. "Katrina, you have helped me in another way."

"And how is that?" she inquired.

"It's been a long time since I have had feelings for anyone. I was happy just being out in the fields and riding my horse wherever I wanted to go. But, the more I'm around you, the more I want to be near you. You bring a certain kind of peace with me. You fill a void I have had for a long time. The times we've been together, even the disagreements we have had, excite me. I'm not sure how to explain it."

Katrina stood there looking at him.

"Well, say something," remarked Jack as the silence seemed like an eternity.

"Well, I'm . . . I think that's the most words I've heard from you all at once or even over a few days!" she smirked and looked up into Jack's eyes. "Jack, you have filled a void in my life, too." There was another moment of silence then Jack cupped his hands around her smooth face and drew her face to face and placed his lips on hers. He pressed softly then the pressure became firmer. Katrina felt like she was melting. Just as soft and gently as he pulled her face toward him, he released her face and moved his hands down to her shoulders. Katrina felt a gentle breeze blow between the two of them. Jack became fidgety and released his hands from her. He thought, *What am I doing. I hope I don't appear to eager. I don't want to push her away. Not now that I feel peace and . . . love. Yes, this feels like love.*

Jack walked over to the fireplace and threw some more logs on the fire.

He turned to Katrina, "I'm sorry. I hope I didn't offend you. I . . ."

"Jack," she turned to look at him, "no apologies needed. I hope that I didn't give you the wrong impression of my feelings. I'm still trying to find myself," she stated as she sat down in the rocker.

Jack went back over to the overstuffed chair and sat down. "Katrina, no wrong impression taken. I understand about finding one's self. I'm doing the same thing. But you have helped me to start figuring it out. Thank you. Can you tell me more about what you want to do with the church? I believe we should have one again in Widow's Peak. What's your idea?" asked Jack with a very relaxed look on his face.

"Jack, I have written and requested my money that I have saved. I would like to use that money to rebuild the church. I have also written for information of having a pastor come to Widow's Peak," commented Katrina.

"You have? Already?" questioned Jack. "Have you spoken to anyone else about this?"

"No, I haven't. Is there a problem?" questioned Katrina.

"No, no I don't think so." stammered Jack. There was a moment of silence as Katrina watched Jack's face. Jack looked at the fireplace then looked back at Katrina.

"Been thinking, what do you think about talking to my father. He'll know what's best and how to get a church back in town. Is that okay?"

"Well," Katrina paused, "that might be a good idea." She went to stand up as she turned to look at Jack sitting in the chair. "Jack, let's wait until tomorrow though, I'm tired."

Katrina went to her bedroom and as she reached the door she looked at Jack. "Jack, thank you, and good night." She entered her bedroom and closed the door.

Jack sat in the chair for a few more minutes while he thought over all that had happened in the last hour. He felt like his world had flipped. He felt refreshed, content and excited. All these feelings, thanks to a woman who entered his life and made a significant impact on him, his family and his world. He looked up and whispered, "Thank you, Lord. Thank you for letting me back into your world and thank you for bringing Katrina to my world. Thank you for making me feel whole again."

Jack headed off to the other bedroom after stoking the fire and turning the lamps down.

Chapter 16

The crimson morning sun was peeking out just above the horizon as Katrina and Jack pulled the horses up to the barn railing and dismounted.

Uncle Tom came running out of the house. "Where have you two been? I've been worried sick," exclaimed Uncle Tom.

"We were at the farm," replied Jack.

"Uncle Tom, we need to talk to you. It's real important, but we need Mr. Whitaker to talk to as well," commented Katrina.

"Well, come on," motioned Tom as he headed to the kitchen door. "Your father, Jack, is in the dining room. Have you two eaten yet this morning?" asked Tom.

They all entered the dining room. Amelia followed them carrying two cups and plates and placed them on the table at the empty end, opposite Mr. Whitaker. Everyone sat down. Jack scooped some eggs on his plate as Amelia poured coffee in his cup. Katrina took a piece of banana bread and buttered it as Amelia poured her a cup of hot tea. Katrina took a sip from the cup, then set it down.

"Well, I . . . I have something to say, actually ask," Katrina spoke up with initial hesitation. She looked at Jack then at Uncle Tom and finally settled her eyes on Mr. Whitaker.

"I have talked with Jack about this and now I would like to get your opinions, directions on an issue that I have a strong belief on. Or should I say a newfound . . . renewed belief."

"What are you talking about," spouted Mr. Whitaker. "Make some sense, girl." Mr. Whitaker then had a snicker on his face. "Sorry, I'm used to folks getting to the point."

"Katrina, go on," encouraged Jack.

"What I'm talking about is getting a church back. The town, community could use a church, don't you think?" Katrina was hoping to involve the others so she didn't have to do all the talking.

Mr. Whitaker sat back in his chair and looked at Tom. "Well, what do you think Tom. Do you believe the town is ready for a church again?" pondered Mr. Whitaker.

Tom replied, "Why not? It might do us all good." He looked at Katrina. "I didn't know you believed in God. What brought this up now?" asked Tom.

"I'm not 100 percent sure. I do know that I have missed the peace I used to have from praying and feel the void from my lost faith. When Jack and I were in town the other day, I saw the abandoned church and I felt a burning inside; a sadness. I wanted to cry out. I felt pain and hurt. It was like all those who used the church were screaming, "Save the church, bring God back." And then talking with Jack last night, it just made me want to do something about rebuilding the church and the faith in Widow's Peak.

Jack intercepted to add on to Katrina's request. "Father, I believe there are a lot of folks who would love to have a church in town. Those who opposed it before, they're all gone now. It's time to rebuild the town."

"I agree!" exclaimed Tom. "I'm in. What can we do to help?"

Mr. Whitaker was still sitting back in his seat. He moved forward and put his elbows on the table. Then he clasped his hands together.

"First thing we have to do is pray!" Mr. Whitaker bowed his head and glanced up to see if the others were ready to pray. As he saw everyone bow their heads, he again put his head down and began the prayer.

"Our Father in Heaven, this has been a long time coming. It took a young lady to come to us to help us open our eyes. The people of Widow's Peak have neglected you for too long. It's time we find our faith and return to you. Please help us to bring your church back. Guide us in opening doors to make this happen. In Jesus' name, Amen.

Tom smiled, "Wow Albert. Didn't know you had it in you. That was a great prayer!" exclaimed Tom.

Katrina spoke up, "I have gone ahead and started the process. I have money set aside to buy the new lumber to rebuild the church building." She didn't think this was the time to mention her inquiry for a pastor.

Jack noticed that she didn't say anything about getting a pastor. He figured she had a reason and he decided to help get his father and Tom thinking on the building.

"So, we need to get to planning the lumber and work details. When and who can help."

Mr. Whitaker stood up. "Let's get a meeting set up with the folks from town and those in the country. I'll ride into town and get the talk started and set up a meeting date, time and location." He went around the table and walked up to Katrina's chair, pulled it out and reached his hands under Katrina's arms and picked her up so she was standing on her feet. He put his arms around her and gave her a big hug. "Thanks Katrina. you have given us a new lease on life."

The town was in a stir. Folks were all out of their homes and walking down the street, riding horses and wagons to the town center which is a big square at the end of the beaten down town where an abandoned building that was once painted white and used to have a steeple at the front center area of the roof.

As Katrina rode up to the square in the Whitaker wagon with Mr. Whitaker and Uncle Tom, she suddenly realized that this gathering of a lifetime to most folks is because of her. She felt excited and nervous at the same time.

Mr. Whitaker pulled the wagon up to the old hitching post in front of the old building and they stepped out of the wagon. Mr. Whitaker went to the platform that had stood in the square for about twelve years. He stood on the boards and raised his hands in the air. As Katrina looked around she noticed more folks gathering around. She had no idea there were this many people in Widow's Peak. She was astonished. Where did they come from? she wondered.

It seemed like an eternity, but after a few minutes, Mr. Whitaker cleared his throat and again raised his hand as he spoke.

"Folks, may I have your attention?" People gathered closer. Many sat on the ground while several stood as Mr. Whitaker started to talk again.

"You all know why we are here. It's been suggested that we rebuild the church and once again bring Christianity back to Widow's Peak. How do you all feel about this?" There's whispering among several folks. Mr. Whitaker again put a hand up to quiet folks.

"How many of you are willing to attend a church again?" he questioned.

As Katrina looked around, the hands, lots of hands, went in the air. She heard folks commenting, "Oh, to have a church would be great." "Church picnics, too." "We'll need new Bibles." "I want to hear sermons again." and many more comments were shared between the crowd of enthusiastic towns folk.

Jack walked over to Katrina's side and whispered in her ear. "Sounds like it's unanimous about Widow's Peak having a church. What do you think?"

Katrina glanced to her side where Jack was standing, "I hope they mean it."

Jack turned her towards him so they were face to face. "Are you getting cold feet now?"

"No, I just want to be sure they want this," stated Katrina as she turned back to see the crowd. She noticed Uncle Tom step on the platform.

He spoke loud so all could hear him. "If you are all serious about wanting a church here, we will need your help, your support."

A man in the crowd shouted out, "Where's the money coming from? That building is going to take a lot of work and supplies."

Another person spoke up, "It sure will, I can give time but I don't have the funds to contribute."

"Neither can I" "nor me" "well, I can't let go of any money, barely feeding my family now." Suddenly, the talk sounded negative. Katrina felt panic crawl up inside of her body. She clutched her chest. Jack saw her movement and he knew she was in pain. He remembered her mentioning having panic attacks. He leaned toward her and said, "It's going to be fine. Remember, you said you had the money. And I have a feeling my father will contribute, too. So, don't worry."

She glanced at him and he winked. That wink made her feel relaxed some.

As Katrina looked back over at the platform, she noticed Mr. Whitaker talking to a group of other ranchers. Uncle Tom was searching through the crowd and noticed Katrina, he motioned for her to come over. Jack saw Uncle Tom and he walked Katrina over to the platform. Mr. Whitaker saw Jack and Katrina approach them.

As Katrina came upon the group gathered near Mr. Whitaker, she noticed that most of the group were business owners from town.

Uncle Tom put his arm around Katrina and guided her to the center of the group.

"Listen up," stated Tom, "my niece is the one who started the talk about a church. She has informed Mr. Whitaker and me that she wants to help with financial funds." Uncle Tom looked around at the crowd and back at Katrina. "We should do a fundraiser. Then folks will feel like they contributed. What do you think, Katrina?" inquired Tom.

"That sounds like a great idea," replied Katrina.

Just then, Constance stepped from behind Mr. Whitaker. She had heard part of the conversation about a fundraiser and interrupted, "I am the person to run it, the fundraiser, that is. I'm the right person for the job."

Mr. Whitaker gasped and said, "Yes, you would be the right one."

"Yes, and I would like to have Jack help me," she smirked.

"Sorry, I'll be busy with the building committee. Can't be in two places at the same time," replied Jack as he walked over towards Tom. "Then we will need to get the measurements," commanded Jack as he put his arms over Tom's shoulder and steered him toward the dilapidated building that used to be the church.

In the meantime, several of the older ladies encircled Constance and they were suggesting a menagerie of ideas for a fundraiser.

Katrina looked at Mr. Whitaker and they both gave a chuckle as they headed back to the wagon. Mr. Whitaker turned towards

Katrina and said, "If only you knew what you are doing for this town. I have not seen these folks so excited and willing to work together in such a very long time."

He leaned closer to her and continued in a lower voice hoping to avoid others from hearing his next words. "Katrina, I also want to thank you for giving Jack hope and life again." He winked at her and then climbed up on the wagon as he grabbed the reins.

Katrina's face turned slightly red, then a puzzled look went across her face. *What did he mean by hope and life?* she wondered. Was there more than what she knew. Then she wondered if Mr. Whitaker knew what Jack had told her.

Suddenly, there was a commotion back toward the square. She turned to look just as she heard Jack yell out, "Stop! Now!" She saw Jack reach out and grab a young boy who was running. Then she saw an elderly man hobbling over to Jack and the boy. Jack had the little guy by the collar.

"Okay Richard, give Mr. Olly back his hat, now." The boy handed a grey dirty hat to the elderly man and lowered his head as he said," I'm so sorry, Mr. Olly. I won't do it again." Jack let go of the boy as he handed the hat back to Mr. Olly. Mr. Olly remarked, "Oh well, I guess it's okay, you were just having some fun." Everyone laughed. At that point, Katrina climbed in the wagon and sat next to Mr. Whitaker.

She felt a breeze, a gust of wind, blow by her face and moved her hair. She said to herself, *Thank you father, and thank you my Father from above.*

On the ride back to the ranch, Katrina explained the funds she had secured and that she was holding the money in the town bank. She said she hoped she had enough money to purchase the lumber needed to build the church.

Mr. Whitaker was surprised to hear how much she had. He reassured her that she had enough money to rebuild and add on to the church.

She asked Mr. Whitaker if it would be okay for her to purchase some Bibles. He looked at her with a smile and responded, "Katrina, don't you think you've done enough already?" He paused, "Let's see if anyone else might want to help by contributing Bibles. If not, then we'll talk." Mr. Whitaker winked at Katrina. "I also believe we need to form a committee and I would like to have you on it. Would you be interested?"

"A committee?" questioned Katrina.

"Yes, about five people to oversee the building process and operation of the Church once it gets going."

"I understand the building part, but the operation? I don't understand."

Mr. Whitaker slowed the horses as they rounded the bend at the Peak. "We don't want someone taking over and manipulating this project. Also, this is for the Lord, our family and the town. We want to be sure the devil doesn't take control."

"Do you really think that someone would be that way?"

"Katrina, as a businessman, I have learned to trust very few folks. Especially when it comes to things that involve other folks," remarked Mr. Whitaker as he picked up the leather smelling reins and snapped them to make the horses start up at a trot. The wagon rolled along the bumpy pathway. Mr. Whitaker continued his one-sided conversation as Katrina listened.

"This church, I can see this church rebuilding this town. We need a kick in the pants to get this town back up on its feet."

Katrina had a starry-eyed look as she responded, "You believe that Mr. Whitaker?"

"Yes, I do, and we need a minister, too!" replied Mr. Whitaker as he looked at her then turned back to the road.

They finished the ride back to the ranch in silence.

The next morning, Katrina felt overwhelmed and antsy, so after breakfast she quietly snuck out of the house and walked to the area of paradise. As she approached the luscious green land surrounded by woods, miniature falls and rocky terrain with a patch of land in the middle, she heard the little stream running through. The bubbling water was peaceful and tranquil with the crystal-clear water pouring over and around the smooth stones. Katrina could hear the gurgling of the water as she found a rock to sit on. She looked around and felt a calmness overcome her. As she prayed to the Lord to thank

Him for this precious moment, this land that she presumed must be like Heaven, she felt once again, a gust of air. It was warm air that surrounded Katrina leaving her feeling like she was being pulled into a hug. A powerful strength came over her as she spoke to the Lord.

"Thank you, Lord, for the reminders of my father and for being in my life. I was lost for a while but have returned. I never thought I could be with you again after all that I have done. This is my cleansing, Lord. Today I release my past wrongdoings and start with a new future. Can I do this, Lord? Will you forgive me? Help me to move on in the direction of peace and contentment, happiness, and tranquility. I believe in you, Lord, and know that you are the one and only to help me with my faith and strengthen it to be even better than ever.

My past, I am not proud of it. The rough life I lived after losing everything, especially my mother who died from a mysterious illness. I don't ask why, but I do thank you for her life she had here and I know she's in Heaven with you, not suffering from the pain she had here on this mortal plane. I know that father sent us east with mother's family so she wasn't in this desolate town. I wonder if she knew about this place. He hoped that the doctors in Philadelphia could help her. But, as mother taught us, God is in control. When you took her and I couldn't and didn't understand that, I hated you for taking her. Please forgive me, Lord. I know now that she is in a better place. That's what everyone said at her funeral. As I searched to understand that, I lead myself down the wrong path. I do hope you forgive me for leaving my brother and sister with our grandparents. I couldn't take them with me and I am glad I didn't. The path I traveled was too rough and they wouldn't have survived. I hope the letters I've been writing to them lets them know I care. Maybe, someday, I can bring them out here to live with me and Uncle Tom. But not before I help the town to become a community again."

Katrina stood up and moved over toward one of the falls. The water dropped about twelve feet down off a flat ledge above and swirled lightly in a pool at ground level. She stepped under the falling water and spoke to the air.

"Lord, please wash me of all my sins, the stealing of food so I could eat, the running from people while looking for a place to sleep at night."

Katrina heard a noise behind her that sounded like a snapping branch. As she turned to look to see who or what was behind her, she noticed a shadow move in front of her. She knew it was someone and that made her panic. She gasped as she swiftly turned her body around. She was looking at Jack. He stood there like a little boy who had been caught doing a prank.

"I'm so sorry Katrina. I was worried about you and then when I thought you might be here and then hearing you talking to yourself . . . are you okay?" asked Jack with a concerned look on his face.

"I was!" remarked Katrina. She was now upset that her talk to her Lord was interrupted.

"I am sorry to interrupt, intrude and . . . and be worried about you," muttered Jack as if he had been reprimanded. "I'll leave, since you are okay and not hurt." Jack turned and started to walk away.

Katrina realized she had hurt him when all he was doing was caring about her. He was concerned. She still was skittish about folks caring. Without further thinking, Katrina begged, "Jack, stop, please. I'm the one who is sorry. You just surprised me."

Jack turned to look at Katrina, "You have nothing to be sorry for, Katrina. I realize now that you were having a time for prayer. I respect that and was going to turn away and leave you alone when the twig snapped."

Katrina stepped out of the water and Jack walked toward her. As she reached the spot where Jack stopped in front of her, she looked up at him. "I can finish my prayers later." She looked down and asked Jack, "Do you believe in the Lord, honestly believe?"

Jack looked up at the sky and then around at the falls and hills. He took Katrina's hands and cupped them in his. "Yes, Katrina. I do now."

"What do you mean, you do now?" inquired Katrina as she moved her hands from his. She noticed a disappointed look in his face.

"Katrina, you aren't the only one who wants this new church. I believe it will bring peace and comfort to many people and bring them back to the Lord again."

Katrina knew he generalized his answers. She knew she shouldn't pry any further, but she felt driven to know what made this handsome rugged man tick.

"Can you tell me why you now believe, Jack?" she questioned, but it was more of a statement. She wanted to know about him.

"Well, I . . . I was lost too." Jack went over to the rock and sat down. "Katrina? Do you really want to know about me?" quizzed Jack.

"Only if you want to tell me." replied Katrina.

"Come, sit here." Jack patted the spot next to him on the large rock that seemed like it was made just for two.

Katrina thought about how that rock didn't seem that big when she sat there before. And Jack said he was trying to leave when the twig made a noise. Are these signs from the Lord? Was the Lord leading them together?

"Katrina," Jack was trying to get her attention. He wondered if he said something wrong. He called her name again and was just about to stand when Katrina walked over and sat down.

They sat there in silence for a minute then they both looked at each other and said simultaneously. "Do you?" They stopped at the same time, then laughed.

Katrina took Jack's arm with both of her hands as she was laughing. Jack looked in her eyes as she looked into his. They both felt a mesmerizing connection between the two of them. Jack leaned forward to kiss her and she didn't pull back. She wanted the kiss as much as he did.

The kiss held a sweet, sensual feeling that lingered after their lips released. But their lips did not separate for very long and once again, they kissed, then touched cheek to cheek, his lips then kissed her cheek and then brushed her skin as they slowly moved to her forehead and paused there with two more puckers on her forehead.

Katrina tingled all over. This was a very special feeling and she didn't want it to end. She didn't pull away. Jack realized that she was enjoying the affection. But he knew he had to stop and stop now. He released her and held her back firmly with both of his hands on her arms and then he looked at her face.

"Katrina, I have realized that I care for you. No, not just care, I . . . I . . . love you. I didn't think I could ever love again. But you are so special."

As Katrina looked in his eyes she responded, "Thank you, Jack. I also love you and I feel the same way. I didn't think I would ever find love."

Jack leaned toward her once again and they kissed as if to seal their pact. They sat there on the rock holding each other and watching the water tumbling down in front of them as if to be mesmerized by the Lord's beauty.

About the Author

L uAnn Henry lives in Western New York with her husband Bob and her cat named Max. Bob has been by LuAnn's side since they were married in 1975. She has two sons who live close by with their growing families totaling eight grandchildren and four great grandchildren. Family and friends are a huge part of her life including her reenacting family. The history of the 1800s is an era that attracts LuAnn and is strongly reflected in her Civil War re-enacting life at the weekend events she and her husband attend.

Joyce, LuAnn's mother, has been her leading supporter for reassurance and assisted LuAnn by typing most of her manuscript. It was a special couple from her historical reenacting, Craig and Sandi, who encouraged LuAnn to follow her passion and dream of writing. With the expertise of an English teacher, Samantha; LuAnn realized that she truly has talent with her writing technique to produce a story worth reading for those interested in a creative Christian romance.

Writing has been a dream of hers since high school, then life blossomed with marriage, two children, and a secretarial/administrative assistant career in a variety of fields such as insurance, public relations, printing and binding industry, and special education. LuAnn has a variety of hobbies including reading, watching movies of many genres, embroidering, civil war re-enacting, and gardening. She has gathered family genealogy records from her parents and her husband's parents as she feels strongly about family understanding their past and knowing about their ancestors to enable a person to know who they are.

LuAnn has a strong belief that the Lord is guiding her every day to keep the faith and giving her patience and creativity of writing fiction to reveal how important it is to share the faith and love of the Lord with her readers. Her writing also presents to her writers the strength of faith when allowed to be a part of a person's life.

CPSIA information can be obtained
at www.ICGtesting.com
Printed in the USA
BVHW061736101218
535226BV00012B/740/P

9 781643 493985